INSISTENT

NEW YORK TIMES & *USA TODAY* BESTSELLING AUTHOR

KAYLEE RYAN

Linda
xoxo
Kaylee Ryan

Cover Design: Perfect Pear Creative Covers
Cover Photography: Scott Hoover
Cover Model: Travis DesLaurier
Editing: Hot Tree Editing
Formatting: Integrity Formatting

INSISTENT

1. Demanding something.
2. Persistent.
3. Compelling attention or notice.

CHAPTER 1

GAVIN

ITTING AROUND THE TABLE AT Soul Records with my bandmates turned business partners, I have to fight to keep my eyes off her.

Cassidy.

I've watched her from afar for years—waiting, biding my time—but there never seems to be a right time. She clams up anytime I even hint at taking her out. I've gotten creative when I'm around her, finding ways to touch her that won't get my ass thrown in jail for sexual harassment.

Nothing too crazy, but a brush against her here, or a hand on her shoulder there. I've learned to stand back and wait so I can guide her into the room with my hand on the small of her back. She has this crazy, wild, blonde, curly hair, and I find myself tucking it behind her ears more often than not. She's become my addiction, one that wants nothing to do with me.

She's attracted to me. I can see it in her sapphire eyes, can hear it in the way her breath hitches when I'm close to her. She feels it, but she's fighting it. She claims we have to maintain a professional relationship, and I get it. I do. At first, she worked for the band on behalf of the label, formerly known as Stone Records. Once all the shit went down and we bought it out, changing the name to Soul Records, she pushed me away.

Technically, owning the label, I was not just her boss because she was assigned to me, but it was my company who paid her salary.

So I've been on the sidelines, waiting, watching, wanting her more as each day passes. I've contemplated talking to the guys, seeing what they think, but they've all got so much going on with their wives and kids, they don't need my single guy drama. This is one I'm just going to have to figure out on my own.

"Gav," Kacen says, pulling my attention back to the meeting. "Did you hear a word I said?"

"Nope." No sense in lying.

He sighs. "There's a band we need to check out. They're big time in their hometown and the surrounding counties. Selling out shows weeks in advance."

"Where are they?" I ask.

"Missouri. St. Louis, specifically," he tells me.

"When?"

"This weekend," Cole answers.

"I'll go," I say. I know the guys hate leaving their families for these kinds of things.

"Thanks, Gav. I think we need two opinions on this one, just to make sure they're a fit for us," Tristan chimes in.

"Good idea," Cole agrees. "Not that we don't trust you, G, but you know, two approvals are better than one."

I look at them quizzically. I have no fucking idea what they're yammering on about. I've done this more times than I can count on my own, since they all settled down and we bought the label. Suddenly they don't trust my judgment? *What the fuck?*

"You know, that might show them we're serious, too. I know there are a few other labels who are shopping them as well," Kacen says, agreeing with this madness.

"Guys—" I hold up my hands, but Cole interrupts me.

"I can't go, not this weekend. T?" he asks Tristan.

"Can't. Little man has a doctor's appointment on Friday. No way am I missing that."

"Kacen?" he asks.

"Jace, Logan's brother, is playing a game against Tennessee this weekend. We're going to the game," he says.

"Cassidy," Cole says. Suddenly, my mind clears and my eyes widen as I focus on what he has to say. "Can you clear your schedule?" he asks.

"Me?" she asks, surprised.

All my efforts to ignore her are shot down with the sound of her sweet voice. Just a hint of southern, but I could recognize the sweet sound anywhere. My eyes are now focused on her, and ideas are running through my head. It will just be the two of us all weekend. This might finally be my chance to convince her we can do this. That the chemistry raging between us could be so much more.

"Yeah," Kacen jumps in. "You've been with us from the beginning. Not just the label, but as a band."

"We know you have good taste." Tristan points to his chest, causing her to laugh.

Her eyes flash to mine. "You sure?" she asks, giving her attention back to my boys.

"Positive," all three of them say at once.

"Gav?" she asks.

I fight like hell to not let my elation show through. "Sure, it's always good to get another opinion." I'm doing an internal fist bump, impressed I didn't lose my shit when they first suggested that I needed someone to go with me. Cole clears his throat, gaining my attention. He grins and winks, and that's when I know that I've done a shit job of hiding the fact that I want her.

I glance at Kacen and Tristan, and they, too, are grinning like fools. I should be pissed off that they're meddling, but I'm not. I need this time away with her, just the two of us.

"Maybe you all should go down a day or two early, scope out some other bands. The music festival is for four days. Should be a good time to check out a variety but only have to make one trip," Kacen tells us.

He's the level-headed business mind, and even though what he says makes sense, I know we're not really in the market for more than one more band. We like to work one-on-one, give them our attention and expertise, so I know he's blowing smoke up our asses.

For me.

My bandmates, they're like my brothers. No matter what gets thrown our way, we have each other's backs. This is just another example of that. Even though I tried to hide it, I couldn't keep the fact that I want her all to myself. They know me better than anyone.

Thinking back, I realize I did a shit job. I was the one who volunteered to get involved more when it was still Stone Records and we were just a band signed under them. I used the excuse of wanting to learn more about the business when, in reality, I just wanted to be closer to her. Over time, I did learn quite a bit, and that knowledge came in handy when all the shit went down with Wilson, and we ended up buying the label. Soul Records was born and my desire for Cassidy Hillman grew tenfold.

"Solid plan," Tristan agrees.

"I'll have Logan take care of the travel arrangements and let you know," Kacen says, standing.

"I can do that," Cassidy rushes to volunteer.

"Nah, she's been complaining we don't use her enough. She'll be glad to do it. I'll be in touch," Kace says, strolling out of the room.

"Thanks for taking one for the team, Gav." Tristan smirks before standing and leaving as well.

"Looking forward to your report." Cole gives me a big-ass grin, and I know that their well wishes are not in hopes of finding a new band for our label, but for me to finally get the girl.

CHAPTER 2

Cassidy

TRAVELING FOR MY JOB IS not uncommon. It's like second nature to me, but this trip, the one I'm currently trying to pack for is different. It's just going to be me and Gavin, and, well… that's nothing but a recipe for disaster. Truth be told, it's taken every ounce of self-control that I can muster to fend off his advances.

The truth is he's so damn gorgeous, all six feet two of him to be exact. Every time I glance at his fine muscular build, I have to fight not to drool. He's perfectly toned, just enough that his T-shirts cling to the defined muscles in his arms and chest. And his hair… hell, his dishwater blond hair is short on the sides and long on the top, making me want to run my hands through it. The image always makes me want to swoon. That teamed with his beard—not a "mountain man" one, but just enough to be sexy as hell, at least on him. But then really, it's his eyes, his mesmerizing blue eyes that really get to me. When locked on me, I feel as though they can see clear to my soul.

I'm in so much trouble.

So the dilemma is packing. What to wear on a four-day excursion with the man you want and who wants you, but whose advances you keep dismissing? I'm torn. I want to look sexy for him, but at the same time, I know I shouldn't do anything to add fuel to the fire. I can't. Mustn't. I've worked too damn hard to get where I am. I love my job. I get along well with all the guys, their wives, and kids. Since Soul Records was established, I couldn't be happier. I was in the market looking for a new job, not because of the industry but because of my skeevy boss. Then one day, Kacen announced they were buying the label, and I breathed a sigh of relief.

I grew up with nothing. When I say nothing, I mean, *nothing*. My mom and I lived in a low-income, run-down apartment. She worked two jobs, and I spent most of my time holed up in our apartment alone heating up macaroni and cheese in the microwave. My dad skipped out on us when I was two, leaving Mom to raise me all on her own. We struggled for years. I busted my ass in school to get a full-ride scholarship, and when I landed my job at Stone Records, it was as if we won the lottery. Mom's health was failing, Alzheimer's, and she needed around-the-clock care. My job allows for that. I can provide for her, placing her in one of the best assisted-living establishments in Nashville and still take care of myself without eating Ramen every meal.

That's why I can't let anything happen with Gavin. I want him, and I won't lie and not admit the attraction I feel for him is nothing I've ever felt before, because the chemistry is off the charts. To make matters worse, he's not an asshole rock star. Rather, he's a genuinely nice guy.

I was making good money before, but when the guys bought out the label, they kept me on, gave me more responsibilities and a hefty pay increase to go with it. It's more than the average market for equal positions like mine. I know that and so do they, but I bust my ass to earn it, even though they make it easy. I can't afford to lose my job or have the awkwardness that comes with it from a hookup. So I've kept my distance.

This trip is going to test my resolve. When I say I want him, that the attraction is there, I mean it burns as brightly as the sun. What I wouldn't give for just one night to forget about all my responsibilities, to let my worries fade into the darkness and see where the night would lead us. That's a dream, well, more like a fantasy that will remain so. Nothing good ever comes from a work relationship, especially with one of your bosses.

Nothing good.

So here I am, back to my original dilemma. How do I pack for this trip? Sitting on the edge of the bed beside my suitcase, I release a heavy breath. I have to get this done so I can visit Mom before we leave in the morning. My heart constricts knowing that more than likely she won't even realize I'm there. This disease is hell. Regardless of if she knows me or not, I still visit her religiously. I believe that deep down she knows. There have been a few days here and there when she recognizes me and even fewer when she's lucid and we can actually carry on a conversation. I live for those days.

My phone rings, pulling me from my thoughts. Glancing at the screen, I see Logan's name. "Hey," I greet her. Logan, Stacy, and Lauren have become great friends of mine over the years. Really, my only friends. I don't have much time for anything but work and going to see Mom. I refuse to let her be one of those people in a home who never get visitors.

"I hear you're going on a trip?" I can hear the smile in her voice.

"Yeah. Gavin has to go check out a band and none of the guys could go, so they elected me."

"You poor thing. You have to spend four days with Gavin."

"He's not so bad," I say before thinking.

"Oh, I didn't mean it as a bad thing. I was actually being sarcastic." She laughs. "Look. For months, hell, the last few years I've watched the two of you dance around each other. You might think you're doing a good job of hiding it, but I see it."

Well, damn. "What you see is me brushing him off."

"Why would you do that? He's a great guy."

How do I explain this to her? "He's my boss."

"Try again, Cassidy. Kace was my boss, too. Look how we ended up."

"That's different. You two had this… connection. You were destined to end up married and with babies. Speaking of, how is baby Drew?" I ask, trying to steer the subject from me and Gavin.

"Drew is perfect, but stop trying to change the subject. Listen, Cassidy. You're my friend, and Gavin, he's family. I've watched him and there's been no one. Not one woman in his life since the day he set his sights on you. I don't know if you see that, but I wanted you to know."

"Thank you, but I just have too much at stake."

"I know you're taking care of your mom, and believe me when I tell you that regardless of how a relationship does or does not turn out with the two of you, you would never lose your job over it." Butterflies swirl in my stomach at her words, but I can't believe them. It's too risky. "So it's really up to you to decide. Take this trip to see how you two can be together. The worse thing that can happen is that you go back to ignoring him when you get back."

"You're supposed to be talking me out of this." I shake my head and laugh.

"Nope. I'm cheering for the two of you. As a matter of fact, we all are."

What? My stomach drops. "Clarify all?" I ask hesitantly.

"All of us. Kace and the guys, all of us wives, hell, I'm sure the kids can even feel the tension rolling off the two of you." Humor laces every syllable.

I groan. "Logan, this is wrong, so very wrong. I can't risk it."

"It's not a risk. Your job is secure. I talked to Kace, Cole, and Tristan last night. They know I'm calling you." My breath hollows out at her words. "We all want to see Gavin happy. We all want to see you happy. This is to let you know that you have our blessing to go for it. See what happens. Hell, maybe after a few days you two will have worked this out of your systems. Actually, I take that back. You've changed him."

My breath stutters. I'm legit struggling to comprehend that not only is everyone talking about the two of us, but that they're actively cheering as well. "Changed him?" I ask, surprised.

"Yeah, you. I assume you're the one he's always texting?"

My mind wanders to all of our messages over the years. That's how I really came to know him. It started out as business and then led to *good morning* and *good night* texts. That led to *how is your day?* and it just progressed from there. Over that time, Gavin became more than just my boss and the man I long for but continue to refuse. He's my friend. One I'm scared as hell to lose over a romp in the sheets.

"We text," I admit.

She laughs. "Cassidy, that man is gone for you. I wish you could see what we see. Take a leap of faith."

Looking over at my still empty suitcase, I think about what she's saying. Can I do this? Can I risk it all? "I don't know what to pack," I confess. "I'm so torn, Logan. I want to look good for him because of the way he makes me feel when he looks at me, but at the same time, I need to not add any fuel to the fire. Gah! I can't believe I just confessed that."

Again, she laughs. "Cassidy, be you. Dress how you're the most comfortable. If I know Gav, he's going to try and take you out since it's just the two of you. Prepare for all scenarios, so no matter what happens, no matter how things turn out, you'll feel prepared."

"Sage advice," I agree.

"Have a good time. Let whatever happens, happen. If you need me, just call. Stacy and Lauren told me to pass on the same. We're all here for you. We know what it's like to fall in love with a member of Soul Serenade."

"Hey, no one said anything about love," I remind her, my eyes wide.

"You didn't have to. Bye," she says and ends the call before I can reply.

Love? Am I that transparent? All this time I thought that I was doing well at hiding my feelings for him. Each and every day it gets harder and harder to say no when he asks me out. With each subtle touch, my body craves him more and more. Gah! I need to get busy. Tossing my phone on the bed, I get busy packing. I do what Logan suggested and cover every scenario. I have lounge clothes, jeans, and T-shirts, dressier items for business meetings, and even a little black dress, just in case. I toss in a couple of sets of matching bras and panties, along with a swimsuit, and call it good. I've stressed over it long enough. I zip up my bag and set it in front of my closet. Grabbing my phone, I check the time. I need to get moving.

I'm just about five minutes away from Mom's assisted living when my phone rings through the car speakers. Glancing at the dash, I see it's Gavin. "Hey, what's up?"

"Just seeing if you wanted some company to go see your mom tonight?" he asks.

See, my best friend. He knows me better than anyone. "I'm actually almost there. Thank you though. You all set for the trip? Anything you need me to do before we leave?"

"Cass, it's all under control. I just got an e-mail from Logan confirming our flight and room reservations. I'll be there to pick you up in the morning around seven. Our flight leaves at nine."

"Okay."

"See you soon." His deep, husky rumble washes over me, and I shiver in awareness. I'm in trouble. So much damn trouble.

CHAPTER 3

GAVIN

OO AMPED UP, I BARELY slept last night. Four days. I get four days alone with her. Just the two of us. Sure, we're working, but not at the label. We're going to be in a hotel, and out at the venue. Four days to show her what we could be together. I've waited and given her time, especially knowing she has a lot of responsibilities on her plate with her mom. I've been with her to see her before. Her car was in the shop and she was distraught. I told her to take mine, she refused. Instead, I agreed to drive her anywhere she needed to go, no questions asked. When she gave me directions to the assisted-living home, I knew then why it was so important. I remember she was quiet, only speaking to give me directions. When we pulled into the lot, she looked at me with tears in her eyes and told me her mom lived there and she had Alzheimer's. Then she climbed out of the car. Stubborn ass that I am, I followed her. Sure, I was overstepping, but to see tears in those beautiful eyes of hers, I had to follow to make sure she was okay.

Turns out it was a good thing I did. Her mom was having a bad day. She screamed and yelled when Cass walked into her room, claiming she was a stranger. Cass turned to rush from the room and ran straight into my arms. She was so lost in her head she hadn't even realized I'd followed her. I held her tightly, letting her cry, giving her as much of my strength as I could. Before that day I wanted her. She's gorgeous, with all that thick, blonde, curly hair. And her sapphire eyes… I swear they could stop my heart. That day, holding her when she needed someone, that moment changed things for me. She was more than just a girl who worked for our label who was easy on the eyes. She made me want to be a better man, a man who she could lean on when times got tough. That day I realized my brothers, my bandmates, were lucky fuckers. At that time, only Kace was married, but Cole was lost in his pursuit of Stacy, and Tristan, although I didn't know it then, was already wrapped up in Lauren.

So, yeah, sleep last night was restless at best.

Grabbing my bags, I pull them out to my truck and head out a few minutes early. I know my girl and she needs her caffeine. Making a pit stop at the local coffee house, I order us both an extra-large black. She's not one to need all the frills in life. I add on a couple of glazed doughnuts as they're her favorite, and a muffin for me, and head to her place.

Pulling up outside her condo, I send her a text, letting her know I'm on my way up.

Me: *I'm here. Headed up now.*

Cass: *No need. I'm good to go. I'll meet you outside.*

No way am I letting her lug her bags all on her own. Hopping out of my truck, I jog to the front door just in time for it to open. Like always, the sight of her takes my breath away. Sounds corny even to me, but it's the truth nonetheless.

"Morning, gorgeous," I say, taking the steps until I reach her and placing a kiss on her cheek. That's something I've made sure to do each day. A simple greeting, harmless really, but it gets my lips against her skin.

"Morning." She smiles.

"Where are the rest of your bags?"

"Just this one, and my carry-on." She points to her shoulder.

I don't know why I'm surprised. Cassidy is not a diva. She is so much like Logan, and hell, even Stacy and Lauren, that it's eerie. None of us wanted a woman in our lives who was full of drama and demands, and it seems as though we've all found that. I just need to convince mine that she's exactly that.

Mine.

"That's yours," I say, pointing to the cup holder housing her coffee. "If you look in the bag, there might be a little something extra for you, too." I wink before starting the truck and pulling out of the drive.

"Caffeine," she sings as she grabs the cup and takes her first drink. "I've only had one cup today, so thank you."

"You're welcome. I've only ever seen you drink it black," I say to keep her talking. Her sweet voice filling the truck.

"Yeah, that's how Mom drank it growing up and I just kind of followed in her footsteps. We didn't have the money for fancy creamers, and Mom said black was fine the way it was. I've actually never tried it any other way."

"It's not real coffee unless it's black," I agree. She's giving me glimpses of her life growing up, and from what I gather, they didn't have an easy time. Picking up the bag, I hand it to her. "Here."

Placing her coffee back in the cup holder, she peers into the bag, and I hear her sigh. "You're too good to me, Gavin." She reaches in to pull out one of the glazed doughnuts. "You want one?" she asks before taking a bite.

I want to pull the truck over on the side of the road and watch her eat it. Pathetic I know, but the truth all the same. "No, I actually had a muffin." I point to the now empty and crumpled-up bag sitting on the floorboard. As far as being too good to her, I would give her the world. If only she would let me.

"So what do we know about this band?" she asks, scrunching up her bag and placing it on the floor next to mine.

"Not much, actually. They sent a demo, Kace liked them and wants us to check them out. He has a feeling we're going to want them and wants to get a jump start before any other labels nail them down."

"Shattered Heart, right?" She clarifies the name of the band we're going to see.

"Yeah."

"I watched some YouTube videos of them last night. They're good. They have a similar sound to you guys," she says, reaching for her coffee.

"Yeah, Kace played the demo for us and I agree. I'm hoping that gives us the upper hand and they'll sign with us."

"Any of the other bands on your radar for this trip?"

Just you. "Nah, not really. Just going to listen and see if any of them stand out. What about you?"

"I took a look at the lineup but didn't go in search of them. I figured we were going to be there, and live is a better depiction of them anyway, so no."

"I was thinking the same thing," I say as I pull into the parking lot at the private airport. The guys offered to drive us, even get us a driver, but the thought of her and me alone in my truck, even though it was a short drive, was what I wanted. I'm going to soak up as much time with her as I possibly can during this trip. This is my shot to show her how things could be between us.

CHAPTER 4

I KNEW WE WOULD TAKE the label's private jet. I've arranged travel for them hundreds of times. However, I didn't think about the reality of what that would mean. I didn't think about Gavin and me being alone, just the two of us. I never considered the fact that he would insist on taking the seat right next to mine, even though there are plenty of others he could occupy.

"I was thinking," he says, turning in his seat to face me. Reaching out, he tucks a stray curl behind my ear. This simple move has become a habit, one that causes my heart to race. "While we're here, we should go on that date I've been trying to convince you of. It's just the two of us. No one here to witness it." He smiles.

Have you ever been on the receiving end of a Gavin McIntosh smile? Let me tell you, this man and his smile can have panties dropping in a matter of seconds.

"Gavin," I sigh. "We've been over this." I knew he would bring it up. He doesn't go more than a day or two without asking me to go out with him. It gets harder and harder to say no. Especially after talking to Logan. I want to scream "yes" from the rooftops, but that's just not possible with everything I have at stake.

"Yeah, we have, but I'm not satisfied with the outcome. Come on, Cass. You know we'd be good together."

"You're my boss," I remind him.

"Who gives a fuck about that?" He leans in close, so close I can feel his hot breath against my skin. "I want you," he whispers.

I swallow hard, steeling my features and hoping he doesn't see how he affects me, how his words affect me. "What happens when you no longer want me?" This is a question that has rolled through my head every time he asks, but this is the first time I've ever actually said them aloud. I'm fearful of the answer, which is why I never voiced it in the past. I'm not blind. I've seen that he's not going out and the women who used to swarm the band are no longer around. Is it the thrill of the chase for him? As soon as the thought crosses my mind, I know that's not it, but I just can't risk it.

His big hand, calloused from hours of strumming his guitar, cradles my cheek. "Baby, that will never happen. There's nothing that could ever make me not want you."

"You don't know that, Gav."

He leans in closer. "I do." His lips graze the corner of my mouth, and I think he's going to finally kiss me, something I've fantasized about for longer than I can remember, but instead, he pulls away, and I have to fight to not show my disappointment. I'm a mess when it comes to him. I want him—there's no denying that—but my future, my mother's future depends on me keeping this job. A sure-fire way to lose it would be to sleep with my boss. I can't do that, no matter how insistent my body is that it's a good idea. I think about my call with Logan, how her and the others are cheering for this to happen. She assured me that the guys are on board as well. I just worry about what happens after. Will I have their reassurances then?

"You're my boss," I repeat. It's a weak attempt at best to dissuade him from his pursuit.

He chuckles. "Cass, did you somehow forget that Kacen married his assistant?"

"No, but it worked out for them."

His hand finds its way back to my cheek. This time it's his thumb that strokes underneath my eye. "You have us failing before we even start. That's not fair, Cass. There's no one but you. For a long damn time, there's been no one for me but you. What do I have to do to make you see that?"

"You know what this job means to me, Gavin. I have more than just me to think about. Mom, she's happy where she is, and is receiving the best care. I can't jeopardize that. I won't."

"I'm not asking you to." His voice is low and gruff. "I know what's at stake here, Cass. Just one date. Let me have that. Give me one night to at least pretend that you're mine."

"I'm sorry," I say, shaking my head at the same time. "I just can't." Tears well up in my eyes and I know he sees them when his eyes turn a dark shade of blue.

"Come here." He guides me to his lap and wraps his arms around me. "Just let me hold you," he murmurs against my ear. "For right now, I just want to hold you."

I let him. I'm too weak to refuse the warmth and safety of his arms. It's not the first time he's comforted me, but it's the first time it's because of the reason we can't be together. I'm usually good at keeping my composure, but he's amped up his game and is relentless when it comes to wearing me down. I want nothing more than to give in, to say yes, and beg him to stay locked in the hotel room with me for the next four days, but that's fantasy. My reality is that my mom depends on me. I grew up with nothing, and this job, I've busted my ass to get here. No way can I ruin that just for a chance at a night or two in his bed.

I just can't do it.

It's what I have to keep reminding myself of, despite the repetition. Maybe if I think that, say it often enough, I'll stay strong.

I don't know how long we sit this way, his arms locked tightly around me, but I'm thankful when the flight attendant interrupts asking if we need anything. I slide off his lap into my own seat, much to his dismay. That's my one and only moment of weakness for this trip. I can't let myself fall any harder.

Taking a big drink from my water bottle, I prepare myself for awkward silence the remainder of the flight. However, that's not at all what I get. Gavin pulls his phone from his pocket, connects to the onboard Wi-Fi, and we watch videos of Shattered Heart, the band we're going to see. We also watch a few of the other bands that are going to be at the festival. Gavin asks my opinion and I give it to him. It's almost as if he knew I needed our normal to get through the rest of the flight.

INSISTENT

The drive to our hotel is short and sweet. Gavin checks us in, while I stand with our bags. Wordlessly, I follow him onto the elevator and to the top floor. My heart starts to race when it dawns on me what's happening.

"Logan, she, uh, got us a suite. Two bedrooms, a kitchen and living room. We have separate bathrooms," he says in a rush.

Logan! She's a sneaky little thing, and I make a mental note to call and yell at her as soon as Gavin is out of earshot. One suite, with Gavin, just the two of us for four days. This trip is going to be harder to get through than I originally thought. How can I resist him when I'm basically living with him?

Damn you, Logan Warren.

CHAPTER 5

A SUITE. LOGAN IS GOING to get a big-ass hug from me when we get home. I need all the help I can get to make Cass see we can be great together. The only downfall will be knowing she's sleeping just feet away. At least if she was in another room, it would be harder to get to her. Now I just have to walk across the living area to the other side of the suite. How am I going to sleep with her so close? My only hope is that by the time we leave here, she'll be in my bed, or me in hers. We can sleep if that's all she's ready for. Being next to her is enough.

For now.

Sliding the keycard into the slot on the door, I push it open and motion for her to go on in. I'm being a gentleman, and if she has to squeeze by me and I get to feel her body pressed against mine even for a second, it's worth it. "Go ahead and pick your room. I'm good with whatever."

"You go ahead," she says, biting on her bottom lip.

Damn, that simple act turns me on. Then again, all she has to do is breathe and I'm ready to go. It's her. Cassidy is my drug. "Really, go for it. I assume they're close to identical, but you pick. I want you to be comfortable. I mean, unless you want to room with me?" I toss it out there. It's a dick move to pressure her, but it's no secret I want her.

"Gavin." My name is a sigh, and even that's sexy as fuck. "You know we can't."

"No. I know that you think we can't, but we can, Cass. I give you my word that your job will not be affected."

"Right." She laughs humorlessly. "We've been over this. What happens when you're done with me, then what? Do you really think we can still work together as if you'd never been inside of me?" she asks. Her cheeks turn pink at her words.

Stalking toward her, I don't stop until we are toe-to-toe. Reaching out, I cup her cheek in the palm of my hand. "If and when I'm ever lucky enough to be inside of you, I can't promise I'll ever be able to let you go." My thumb swipes gently across her cheek as she sucks in a breath. Slowly, I drop my hand and step away from her. "Go pick your room. We can then grab some lunch."

I stand still and watch as she collects her bag and wheels it to the room on the right. She disappears behind the closed door without a word. I know she's affected by me, I know that she wants this, but she gets lost in her head in the what-ifs. Fuck, Kacen and Logan did it, so we can, too. I meant what I told her. I don't know that I will ever be able to let her go. For her to worry about what would happen if we're no longer together, that's not an issue for me. It's not even on my radar. I've wanted her for so long, it's almost as if it's just a fantasy. *She* is my fantasy. I know her reservations, the worry about being able to take care of her mom. I just don't know how to calm those fears. How do I show her what we can be, what she means to me?

After grabbing my bag, I drop it on the bed in the second room. It's large, with a king-size bed in the center. A large shower and a separate tub that's big enough for two is off to the side. It's definitely big enough for me and Cass. Shaking out of my thoughts, all too aware I sound like a horny teenager, I quickly unpack and head back out to the living area. She walks out of her room at the same time. "Hungry?" I ask.

"Definitely. The festival doesn't start until tomorrow, so I guess we have the night off."

"You trying to get out of eating with me?" I tilt my head, teasing.

"N-no, that's not what I meant. Just that we didn't have to go to the festival after we eat."

"Let's get you fed. We can figure out what to do with the rest of the day while we eat." We've shared countless meals, but none of them have I been able to hold her hand under the table. I don't get to sit next to her in a booth, my thigh pressed against hers. I don't get to drive her home and kiss her goodnight. One of these days, I'll get to do all those things, when we have our official first date.

Nodding, she heads toward the door. I catch up with her and place my hand on the small of her back, leading her out of our suite and into the elevator. "What are you in the mood for?"

"The hotel has a few restaurants. Let's just pick one of those."

That's Cassidy. No fanfare, no drama, and no bullshit. She's not into the glam of her job or the fact that she's here with me. Just one more thing on the long list of things I love about her. Luckily, for the most part, fans leave us alone when we are out. On the occasion when it happens, Cassidy is the first to back away from the limelight. She's been photographed before, but they know who she is. She was in the public eye when she was working for Wilson when the label was Stone Records, so she's used to it, but she doesn't crave it. That's the huge difference.

"How about there?" She points to a bar and grill in the hotel as we exit the elevator.

My hand finds its way to the small of her back once again, and I guide her to the entrance. "Two," I tell the hostess. With a polite smile, she takes two menus and asks us to follow her. I have to bite down on my cheek to keep my smile at bay when she leads us to a dark corner booth. I wait until Cass is seated before I slide in the seat across from her. I almost moved in to sit beside her, but I've already pushed my luck. Not to mention I don't want to force her into this, into the idea of us. I want her, and I know she wants me, but I know when to back off.

Cass opens her menu then moans. "Bacon cheeseburger." She grins. "And some fries." She closes the menu and clasps her hands on top of it on the table. "What about you?"

I'm still stuck on the moan. What I wouldn't give to have her under me, on top of me, beside me, anywhere, and making that sound. "Yeah, me too," I say after clearing my throat. By the time the waitress stops by to take our order, I have myself under control—well, at least from what they can see. My cock is hard under the table, begging for more of her moans.

"So what are you thinking for tonight? I mean, you can do your own thing. I can hang out in the room if you have plans," she says.

Like I would plan anything without her. "Anything that I do involves you being with me. I thought we could do the tourist thing. Maybe cruise by the arch. I'm not sure if it's operating, but you can go up in it and get a great view of the city, at least that's what my research said. There's also a graffiti wall I'd like to see while we're here. Maybe we should get some spray paint and add our names or something?"

"Is that even legal?"

"It is. I guess it's this huge wall and people come from all around to tag it or whatever it is they call it. The pictures I saw online were pretty great to think they did it with a can of spray paint."

She nods. "I'd like to go see it. Not sure about adding my name but it sounds like something cool to see."

"The festival starts tomorrow, and even though the band we're here to see doesn't play until the day after, I'd still like to go and check out the talent."

"That's why we're here."

"Technically, we only need to see Shattered Heart, and any other bands that we bring back to the group are just a bonus. Is there anything you wanted to do while you're here? Any St. Louis bucket list items?" I ask.

She chuckles. "Not off the top of my head. I'm up for anything."

"Anything?"

"Gavin." While there's a small reprimand in her tone, her smile is blinding as she rolls those sapphire eyes at me.

"Just checking." I grin across the table at her. I crave this time with her. Just the two of us. No matter what happens while we're here, at least I'll get a few days of just Cass. That's more than I can ask for at this point. Maybe, just maybe, I can convince her that what I'm offering is real.

A man can dream.

CHAPTER 6

 Cassidy

I KNEW THIS WAS GOING to be a challenge, but Gavin is pulling out all the stops. He's also his normal charming self, with gentle touches and once again, those eyes. I could get lost in his eyes. I want to, oh how I want to. It's hard to pretend to be unaffected by his words and his subtle caress when all I want is more.

I crave more.

"So where to?" I ask, pushing my plate away. I managed to devour my burger and most of my fries, and I'm stuffed.

Reaching out, he snatches a fry from my plate. "I'm thinking we start at the arch. That way we can take our time at the graffiti wall."

Gavin hands his card to the waitress for our meal. I don't bother arguing. I learned a long time ago anytime one of the guys from Soul Serenade are with you, trying to pay is useless. Besides, this is a business trip and I know the label will reimburse him. "Ready?" he asks, placing his card back into his wallet and sliding out of the booth. He holds his hand out for me and I take it.

It's these little touches, the moments when I can pretend that he's mine and I'm his that I crave. It's innocent enough, friendly, polite, but I can't help but wonder if I'm ever able to give in to this attraction we have for one another, what would it feel like then? To know that when he's touching me, it's because we're one? I've had fantasies, and I can almost guarantee they don't even come close to how it would feel in real life.

"Are you afraid of heights?" he asks once we're back in our rental SUV and on the road.

"I'm not exactly a fan, but I can deal with it."

"What does that mean? Not exactly a fan?"

"It means that by choice, I like to keep two feet on the ground, but I'm not going to let my fear keep me from experiencing something phenomenal."

"Does the St. Louis arch count as phenomenal?"

If it's with you it does. "It's a new experience, and you never know when phenomenal is going to happen."

He chuckles at my reply but doesn't comment. "There is it." Gavin points to the arch that stands tall above the buildings. "You sure you're up for this?"

"We go up in that?" I try to keep my voice from quivering.

"Yeah, I guess there's an elevator that takes you to the top."

"It's safe?" Leaning down, I peer through the front windshield, trying to get a better view.

His hand on my leg startles me. I jump at the contact and turn to face him. "I won't let anything happen to you," he says, tracing my thigh with his thumb.

"That's a great sentiment and all, but you can't keep the elevator from falling."

"No, I can't. But I'd never put you in a situation that I didn't feel was completely safe. We don't have to go up if you don't want to."

"Can I get back to you on that?" I ask as he steers us into the parking lot.

"Let's just go walk around, take in the river. We can decide later if you want to go up."

"I can wait for you if you want to go," I say as we climb out of the SUV.

Gavin waits for me as I walk to meet him on the other side of the car. When I'm within touching distance, he reaches out and places his hand on the small of my back. The warmth of his touch seeps into me. It's hot as hell today, but that's nothing compared to how my temperature rises anytime his hands are on me. The simple touch of his palm to my back has my body overheating. "I'm not doing it without you, Cass. We can do it together or not at all. I'm not going to be heartbroken if I don't go."

"You sure about that?" I tease, trying to lighten the mood and forget about my fear.

"Trust me. The choice is an easy one. Stay on the ground with you or go up without you…. I choose you every time."

His words cause a melting feeling in the pit of my stomach. He started making his feelings known about a year ago. He doesn't hold back from letting me know he wants there to be more between us. Honestly, it's a miracle in and of itself I've held out considering everything he says. He can wax poetic and turn me into a gooey, swoony mess. Then again, he is a musician. That's what he does. He writes and performs music, stringing together lyrics that touch your soul. Soul Serenade is the perfect name for them. No matter if it's a ballad, or a faster base pounding in your chest track, the lyrics touch your soul.

Gavin's hand drops from the small of my back as we get closer to the crowd. For a split second disappointment settles in my stomach, that is until he laces his fingers through mine and pulls me close to him, guiding us through the small crowd. I know I should pull away. The lines can so easily be crossed without much effort from either of us. We just… fit. We get along, have the same tastes in music. We can spend hours talking about everything and nothing. From text messages to chatting at the office, and phone calls, literally everything with Gavin comes easy. Too easy. So much so that I have to remind myself he's not mine, no matter how much we both want him to be.

"Not much to see," he says, his lips next to my ear.

I tilt my head back and shield my eyes from the sun, even though I'm wearing sunglasses. The arch is high, so damn high I can feel my stomach drop at the thought going up in what I'm sure is a tiny elevator. "It's up there," I say, feeling panic start to set in.

"I'm right here." He pulls me closer.

His body is aligned with mine. Here, away from the office, it's hard to remember why I can't just let go and be with him. See where this attraction takes us. This trip is already testing my resolve. "You sure this is safe?" I ask him again, searching for reassurance.

"Look." He points to our right and there's a family of four coming up the steps from the underground elevator. The kids are smiling and laughing and the parents are as well. None of them look traumatized by the event.

I swallow hard. "I can't."

"Then we won't," he says, kissing my temple. "Let's go walk along the river's edge."

So that's what we do. Hand-in-hand we walk along the concrete path that runs parallel with the river. The warm breeze blows through my hair as the sun shines down on us. Gavin's hand is warm wrapped around mine while his shoulder brushes against mine as we walk. We stop to watch a barge pass by and I close my eyes. This is one of those moments where I like to pretend he's mine. I can't help but wonder if he does the same thing.

"Ready for the graffiti wall?" he asks.

"You sure you don't want to go up?" I point to the arch. "I really don't mind waiting."

"And miss time with you? Nah, I'm good." I want to be brave for him. I want to tell him that we can go up, and not be afraid, but the fear coursing through me won't allow it. Instead, I let his words soothe me. Gavin puts me first and, in my limited experience in the dating world, that's a rare find.

We turn and head back to the SUV. Relief races through me that we don't have to go up in the arch. I hate that he's missing out on the experience, but I'm grateful he didn't pressure me to go either. I'm a rapid mix of emotions. I just don't know which is stronger. Gavin opens the door for me and waits until I'm buckled in before shutting the door. I close my eyes and rest my head back against the seat. I know I should tell him to stop. Any other time I would have already. The touches, the kiss to my temple, his sweet words... he's never come on this strong all at once before. I need to tell him to stop, but I can't form the words.

Deep down, I don't want him to ever stop.

And that right there is the problem.

CHAPTER 7

WHY IN THE FUCK HAVE we not gone on a scouting trip before now? I'm kicking myself in the ass for not thinking of it. Leave it to Kace to come up with the idea. If things go my way, if I can convince Cassidy to give us a try, I'll never hear the end of it. That's okay though, because I'll have the girl. He can gloat all he wants. If she's mine, I doubt I'll even hear him.

Glancing over at Cassidy, I see her eyes are closed, head tilted back. Does she realize what she does to me? That I want nothing more than to lean over this console and trace the column of her neck with my tongue? With my hands gripping the wheel, I pull out of the lot.

"How far is the wall?" her soft voice asks from beside me.

"Not far." I glance at my phone where I pulled up the address. "Says ten minutes."

"Did you get paint?"

"Nah, I figured we could see what it's all about first. I'm not much of a painter, and from what I hear, these tags or murals or whatever they're called are pretty badass."

"So, it's legal, people just go and paint this wall?"

"Yeah, from what I read, people travel from all around just to show

27

off their graffiti skills. Sounds pretty cool."

"How big is it?" she asks, and I chuckle which causes her to turn and look at me.

"I can show you." I wink.

"Stop." She smacks my arm, laughing. "How big is the wall?"

"The wall, got ya." I act as though I was confused, but we both know better. "I'm not sure. It's pretty big. Online they said you can walk the wall or drive it, so I assume it's a pretty decent size."

"Hmm," is her mumbled reply as her fingers fly over the screen of her phone.

"Work?" I ask.

"Yeah, the contractors are coming to renovate the top floor. Just confirming dates for next week."

When we took over the label, the top floor was all offices. We're a tight-knit group and none of us really require our own space. There are three large conference rooms on the first floor. We converted one of those to an office space. The entire perimeter of the room is desk space, and we each have our own little area. With our growing families, we decided to make the top floor Soul Serenade only. We're putting in a full kitchen and dining area big enough for all of us, and plenty of room for high chairs, which seems necessary with the way this group is going. We're also adding a huge living room. When I say huge, I mean *huge*. The plans are for one entire wall to be an entertainment center that will more than likely only ever see Disney movies. A large bathroom because with the little ones running around, you never know when a bath is going to be needed. There are four large sectional couches, one for each family. It's important for our group's wives and kids to be there with them. Our hours can be crazy, and it helps to have the ones you love close. Although I'm the odd man out, I agree with this plan wholeheartedly. Besides, it's not by choice I'm still unattached. I'm still waiting on my girl to get the memo that she's that. Mine.

"Wow," I say as I pull up to the stop sign. The wall is just ahead, and although I can only see a fraction of it, I can already tell this is more than just graffiti.

"That's… more than graffiti," she says, mimicking my thoughts.

"That's badass is what it is." I pull up in front of the wall and roll down the window. "You want to walk or drive?" I ask her.

She points out the front window. "I'm thinking drive. This looks pretty long and these shoes…." She indicates her wedged looking heels that look uncomfortable as hell, but make her legs and ass look fucking incredible.

"Drive it is." I creep along, stopping every few feet to look at a new section of wall. The colors are vibrant, and the designs are in a word, incredible.

"Yeah, I'm glad we skipped out on the paint." She laughs. "This is not what I was expecting. These are unbelievable." She leans over the console to look out my window, her pert breast pressing against my arm.

"Looks like someone wanted to add their own spin." I laugh, pointing to the dick that's drawn over an incredible design.

"Some people just have to ruin everything," she huffs.

We continue to slowly drive by the wall, taking in the art, because the talent that adorns this brick wall is astonishing. Cass stays in her spot, leaning over the console, and I have to focus on the wall, the colors, and her words to keep my cock from springing to life. To be honest, it's not working. Luckily, she's more interested in the wall and not what's in my pants, begging for relief, begging for her. All she has to do it look down and there'd be no hiding it.

When we reach the end of the wall, I turn the SUV around and drive back so that the wall is now on her side of the car. She quickly turns in her seat and rolls down her window. "These people, they have real talent. I wonder if any of them make a living out of it? You know, something more than just painting random walls and train cars in different cities. It's a shame to waste that kind of talent. They could be like me." She laughs.

"What?"

She turns to look at me. "I have no talents. I'm not musically inclined. I can't draw a good stick figure. Nothing."

"Everyone has a talent."

"Okay, Mr. I Play Bass for the Hottest Rock Band Around."

"It doesn't have to be music or art. You're organized to a fault, smart as hell, and beautiful," I say.

"Those are hardly talents, Gavin."

"Who says? And what about those books you're always making?"

INSISTENT

"My scrapbooks? That's just a hobby. It started as a way to preserve memories. Mom on her good days would tell me stories, and I would try to capture those on the page with the pictures. It's history, all that I have of my family," she replies softly.

"Yes, those books and they're ridiculously good, Cass. You need to give yourself more credit."

"I use a machine, made for scrapbooking."

"So, I use a guitar. That's a tool of your trade. These painters"—I point to the wall—"use paint."

"I'm not going to win this one, am I?" she asks.

"Not a chance." I laugh.

She smiles softly, her sapphire eyes sparkling. The sun is starting to set over the wall, and it's a backdrop for her beauty; they both are. "I don't know how you do it, but you can almost make me believe it," she says quietly, so much so that if I were not watching her lips, giving her all my attention, I might have missed it.

"Good." Reaching out, I tuck a curl behind her ear. "You've had some tough times, but I hate that you can't see yourself the way that I see you. Beautiful." I let my fingers trail down her cheek. "Smart, loyal, crafty." I grin.

"It's moments like this that make resisting you even harder," she confesses. My heart beats a little faster at her admission.

"Then don't."

"Gavin, we've been over this. You know my reasons."

"I do, and I don't agree with them."

Reaching out, her hand rests against my cheek. "I wish I could give in to this, Gav. More than you know, but there's too much at stake. Not to mention…" She swallows, her eyes boring into mine. I wait, letting her collect her thoughts. "You're my best friend, Gavin. The thought of losing you terrifies me more than that damn arch."

"I promise you, you'll never lose me," I say. My eyes are locked on hers, willing her to see the truth in my words.

Her gaze searches mine, then lands on my mouth. When they flick back up, I can see it. Something's changed, something so incredible that I can hardly believe it. I'm not sure I even dare to.

Then she says, "Let's do it." Her voice shakes, and I fight the elation

30

I suddenly feel. I'm about to lean in to kiss her when she continues. "I need to live a little. Let's go up in the arch." Her eyes are lit with excitement, and I try not to let my disappointment show. "You think they're still open?"

I control my reaction, focusing on her eagerness instead of the crazy beat of my heart. "Only one way to find out," I say, reaching for my seat belt. Glancing over at her, I see she's done the same. Punching the address into my phone, we start the short drive that will take us back to the arch. I know it's crazy to feel rejected as her refusal is not new, but my heart fractures a little, and I'm no longer convinced anything will ever change. I hate that she feels this, wants us to happen as badly as I do but won't give in. I loathe that she fights it.

What will it take to get her to see she's all I want?

CHAPTER 8

I FEEL TERRIBLE. I SAW the way his face lit up, the smile that he was fighting to contain, and then I finished what I was saying, and the happiness gave way to disappointment. I hate it, but I'm not brave enough to change it. I meant what I said. We're friends, and I don't want that to change. The unknown and the worry keep me holding my ground. I want him. They say close friends become the best partners, but that's a risk I can't take. Not with the responsibilities of taking care of my mom. I won't risk losing my means to do that just to satisfy my heart. I'll make the sacrifice.

"You sure you're up for this?" he asks, pulling into the parking lot of the arch.

"No." I smile. "But I want to. I need to overcome this fear. I mean, there were kids doing it so I can do this." I steel my resolve and climb out of the SUV.

Gavin meets me in front of the SUV and laces his fingers through mine. "I'll be right there with you, Cass. I promise you if I thought it wasn't safe, no way would I let you go up in that thing." He points to the arch.

His words melt my heart in typical Gavin style. I nod. "Let's do this before I chicken out and change my mind."

We head toward the ticket booth, and the crowds that were here earlier are gone. The sun is setting over the river. "Two please," Gavin says.

"You made it just in time," the older gentleman tells us. "Nothing like the view at sunset." He hands us our tickets and instructs us to head down the steps toward the elevator.

"Looks like it's just going to be us." Gavin places his hand on the small of my back and leads me into the elevator, if you can even call it that. It's a tiny little space with seats, and it looks more like a tube.

"Just us," I say, trying to sound a hell of a lot more confident than I feel.

"I'm right here." He guides me to sit next to him. His arm wraps around my shoulders and he pulls me into his chest. "I've got you. Just breathe, baby."

If I weren't already freaking the hell out, and trying not to show it, I would be freaking out from his term of endearment. He doesn't address me with them often, but when he does, it makes my heart flutter in my chest. Just like when he calls me Cass. Sure, other people have shortened my name, but no one says it the way he does.

The door closes, and we immediately begin to move. My knees bounce up and down, my palms sweat, and my heart races. I can't believe I'm doing this.

"Hey." Gavin uses the hand that's not wrapped around me to gently grasp my chin and turns me to face him. "I'm right here. We're fine. Just take a deep breath." He waits for me to suck in a gulp of air, but instead of releasing it, I hold it. "Breathe, baby. You have to breathe for me. Damn it, I should have never let you do this." He turns in his seat to face me. Both of his hands cup my face. "Cass, baby, you have to breathe. We're okay, I promise." His voice is pleading.

I nod, and let out a gush of air, only to suck in another gulp. I feel like I might be hyperventilating, but I can't gather myself to tell him, to calm the hell down.

"Please," he whispers. "I need you to breathe." When I don't, he mutters something, then leans in and presses his lips to mine. I'm so shocked I gasp, which just gives him the opportunity to slide his tongue past my lips. Slowly, his tongue explores my mouth while his hands tenderly hold my face, holding me close to him. Suddenly, all I can think about is that this is our first kiss. Sure, there have been pecks on the cheek, he's kissed my temple, my forehead, my hands, even the corner of my mouth, but this, this is the first time his lips have been fully pressed to mine. The first time we've tasted each other. There's a hint of mint and something that I assume is solely Gavin. When he pulls away, I want to protest. Instead, I open my eyes and find him staring back at me.

"That's better," he whispers. With one more quick peck to my lips, he stands, offering me his hands, and I realize we've made it to the top. When the doors open, it's like a long hallway with rows of windows. It's deserted. "Come take a look," he says, guiding me, our fingers laced together to the row of windows facing the river.

"Wow," I breathe. The sun is setting on the horizon and the view is spectacular. Swirls of orange, blue, purple, and gold fill the evening sky. The remnants of the sun are casting a shimmer over the river. "Beautiful," I whisper.

"Yes." He steps up behind me and wraps his arms around my waist.

I know I should step away, but I can't seem to find it in me to do it. Instead, I lean back, resting my head against his chest. "I would have missed this," I say. My words have a double meaning. The sunset at this level is spectacular, but nothing compares to the warmth, the security of having his arms wrapped around me. My lips are still burning from his kiss. I can still taste him, and it would have been a damn shame to have never experienced any of it.

"How do you feel?" His hot breath is next to my ear.

"Better." I don't tell him that wrapped in his arms with the taste of him still on my lips the fear has diminished. "I'm just not really looking down." I chuckle. "Keeping my eyes on the sunset." We stand here, gazing out at the Crayola sky, his arms tight around me, my head resting back against his chest for what feels like hours.

"What time do they close?" I ask as the sun falls farther into the horizon.

"Not sure."

I turn in his arms, placing my hand on his shoulders. He pulls me close, his hands resting on my hips. "Thank you, Gavin. I'm sorry I freaked out."

His eyes soften.

He leans in.

His lips meld with mine.

Lost.

I get lost in him and the feel of his mouth against mine. He traces my lips with his tongue, and I open for him. Without hesitation. I'm not sure what's come over me, but I can't fight him right now. Not with my emotions raw from fear and from being here with him wrapped around me, the scenery, all of it. I can't fight it.

We kiss until we hear a throat clearing, letting us know our time is up, that this bubble we're in is no longer floating. Gavin rests his forehead against mine. "Better than I imagined."

"You imagined me freaking out?" I ask, trying to lighten the mood.

"No." His lips replace his forehead as he kisses it tenderly. "I've imagined kissing you, hundreds, no, make that thousands, possibly millions of times, and I can report that nothing I imagined could be better than the real thing."

"I'm sorry, but we're closing," the attendant says after clearing his throat once again.

With a heavy sigh, Gavin pulls away, laces his fingers through mine, and guides us to the elevator. The attendant joins us, and this time, I don't panic. My legs bounce up and down, but the warmth of his hand in mine keeps the panic at bay. Maybe it's the phantom feel of his lips against mine, but whatever it is, the ride down is quick and without drama on my part. Gavin leads me to the SUV and opens my door for me. He waits until I'm buckled in before closing the door and racing to the other side.

"You hungry?" he asks.

"Not really. I'm still stuffed from our late lunch."

"I'm thinking about swinging through a drive-through and grabbing something. I'll get a little extra in case you change your mind." Reaching over, he laces his fingers through mine, and I contemplate pulling away, but can't seem to find the strength. I can pretend this is real, that this is us and our new reality just a little bit longer.

CHAPTER 9

GAVIN

PULL INTO THE LOT of the hotel and shut off the engine. I don't want to get out of the vehicle. I don't want whatever magic that was cast upon us today to end. She let me kiss her. She kissed me back. I've held on to her hand the whole journey, only letting go to pay for our food. I don't know what any of this means, and I feel like a pussy for even thinking that way, but this is Cassidy, and I want her. I crave her. I don't know how I'm going to pull back now that I've tasted her.

"Ready?" she asks. Her eyes are bright and her smile is, too. She's trying to act unaffected, but I can see it in her eyes. She's worried, which means any hope of continuing what we started in that arch is out of the question.

"Yeah." I reach for the bag of food I set down on the back seat and climb out.

She's waiting for me at the front of the vehicle, her hands in her pockets. Locked out, just as I thought. "That smells good," she says, nodding toward the bag in my hands.

"Best late-night meal ever." I hold up the Taco Bell bag. She laughs, and the sound washes over me. I want to wrap my arm around her and pull her close more than anything, but her body language tells me no.

Instead, I settle for walking close to her, my shoulder brushing against her as we walk through the automatic doors of the hotel. Once we're in the elevator, she pushes the button for our floor and leans against the wall. "Tired?" I ask her.

"A little."

She doesn't give me much, and I know her well enough to understand that she's in her head bitching at herself for letting things go as far as they did. I don't say anything. Instead, I choose to watch her as she closes her eyes and relaxes her stance. She's gorgeous. I could stare at her all day, all night, and never want to look away. I can still remember the day I met her for the first time. She was following that fuckwad Wilson around. Her hair, the long locks of thick curls and those eyes— I was captivated by her. Back then, I was more worried about quantity over the quality of women. Slowly, my bandmates, my brothers started settling down, and quantity was no longer as appealing.

I remember watching Kacen struggle with wanting Logan. At first, I didn't understand it. Then I came to know her and witnessed the two of them together. That's when I knew I wanted what they had. Next came Cole and Stacy, which was a sight to see... to watch him fall for her.... We all thought he would be the last to settle down. Now they have baby Riley who's just a few weeks old, and they couldn't be happier. Then Tristan set his sights on Lauren, and we got baby Zach in the process. Fuck, but I love that kid. I love all their kids, but Zach, he and I bonded when he was born, letting Tristan be with Lauren. It was touch and go for both of them for a while, and Tristan couldn't be in two places at once. So, I stayed in the nursery with the baby while he stayed with his wife. He's my little dude. I hope that when I have kids, they're like him. Hopefully, that can be sooner rather than later. I want all our kids to grow up together like we did. If only I could get Cass on board. She's the only one I can see myself settling down with. I can picture it so clearly, our kids. A little girl with all Cass's blonde curls. The elevator doors slide open, and shaking myself out of my thoughts, I follow Cassidy to our room. She pulls her key out and opens the door.

"I'm going to go take a shower," she calls over her shoulder, not bothering to look back at me.

I set the Taco Bell bag down on the table and decide a shower is exactly what I need. I need to relieve the tension, and my cock is aching from our earlier encounter. I would much rather it be her instead of my hand that's offering the relief, but I'm not complaining. I'll take any piece of her, any chance to hold or kiss her that she'll give me. In time, I just hope I can win her over.

In my room, I strip down, turn the shower to hot and let the steam fill the room. My mind immediately goes to Cassidy, who's also currently naked and wet, just across the suite. Mere feet away from me. My cock is steel from the thought alone. Climbing under the spray, my hands rest against the wall while I hang my head, letting the hot water rain down on me. I wish I knew what to do. What I could do or say to prove to her that us being together is okay.

No longer able to take it, I fist my cock and squeeze, stroking from root to tip. I can still taste her, can still feel the curve of her body, her warmth wrapped in my arms. I stroke faster, harder as images of her naked, wet body flash through my mind. I've never seen it, but I've seen her in some tight clothing and last summer she was at a barbecue at Kacen's. She wore this tiny little purple bikini that brought out her sapphire eyes. It took Herculean effort to keep my eyes and hands off her. I wanted nothing more than to drag her into the pool house, or the bathroom, or fuck... to the side of the house, anywhere away from prying eyes and rub my hands all over her sexy body.

That image does it. I lose control, biting down on my lip to keep from calling out her name. Then again, maybe if she heard me...? Resting my forehead against the wall, I catch my breath. My cock is sated for now, but my heart still yearns for her.

Turning off the shower, I dry off and grab a pair of gym shorts, I don't bother with underwear as I'm going to bed soon anyway. I wander out to the living area and find Cass unloading the bag of tacos.

"Hungry?" I ask. She looks up, her cheeks turning a pale shade of pink. It's easy to see with her wet hair piled up on top of her head.

"They smell so good." She smiles, glancing away.

"There's plenty," I say, grabbing two bottles of water from the fridge and handing her one. Silently, we eat, neither one of us willing to break the ice and talk about today. I don't want to talk about it because I don't want to hear her tell me it was a mistake. I'm sure her reasoning for silence is similar and she doesn't want to hear me tell her it wasn't. We're at an impasse.

"Thank you for today," she says softly. "It was nice to hang out with you."

INSISTENT

Nice.

Nice is the weather we had.

Nice is this room we're in.

Today was more than nice. "Just nice?" I ask before I can stop myself.

"Gavin." My name falls from her lips, those luscious lips that were pressed against mine not long ago.

"You were in my arms, Cass. I was holding you, kissing you. That is a hell of a lot better than nice. Extraordinary is more like it."

"You're right," she agrees. "But, Gavin, you know we shouldn't have crossed that line."

"I disagree. I think we should have and we should do it again, very soon. Nothing has ever felt as right as you in my arms when we watched that sunset. Nothing, Cassidy."

She closes her eyes as if trying to avoid me and my truth. Reaching out, I lace her fingers with mine. I wish she was looking at me, but I know she can hear me. She can hide for now. "I want you, Cass. This isn't just a mission to get my dick wet." Her eyes widen and her breathing accelerates. "I enjoy spending time with you. We both enjoy the simpler things in life, like that sunset we watched earlier. I can see us going to festivals, enjoying the bands, sampling the food."

A small smile tilts her lips. This is something we both enjoy and have done as a group, but never just the two of us. Tomorrow will be a first, and I can't wait for it to just be the two of us.

"I see us lasting. I want you for more than one night."

Her eyes flutter open. "Gavin, this is so hard for me. You're amazing, and I know there are millions of women who would give anything to be sitting here with you. I feel it. I feel the connection, the way my hand tingles when entwined with yours. The flurry of desire anytime you're even in the same room with me. I feel it all, Gavin. But I need my job. You know this. It's important to me. My mom depends on it. We struggled. There were days when we didn't know where our next meal was coming from. Mom busted her ass to keep a roof over our heads, gave up so much to give me all she could."

A tear slides down her cheek, making me feel like a tool for pushing her. "I'm sorry," I say, wiping at her cheek with my thumb.

She laughs humorlessly. "Don't be sorry. Never be sorry for being honest and open. Saying no to you, turning away from this… desire that

I feel for you is the hardest thing I've ever had to do. I've lived through some rough times, and they pale in comparison to how much it hurts my heart saying no to you."

Sliding out of my chair, I drop to my knees. In one quick move, I have her chair pushed back, and I'm between her legs, my hands on her hips. "Trust it, baby. Trust what you feel, trust me to be there for you."

"I'm sorry, I just… can't. I can't risk her care. Not after everything she sacrificed for me. I can't."

I nod. Leaning in, I rest my head in her lap, and she immediately runs her fingers through my hair. We fit, like two pieces of a puzzle. She feels it, wants it even, but she's scared. I need to work harder, stop hiding, and put it out there. She needs to know she's all I see, that I want only her. I would never pressure her into anything, although my heart pleads for me to. I just have to do better at showing her that this isn't a game to me; it's not the chase I want. I just want her.

Only her.

Lifting my head and my hands, I cup her face. "I'll show you, baby. I'll show you we can be together. I'll show you," I say, my voice soft. She leans into me, and I can't stop my lips from pressing to hers.

She pulls back, a look of sadness and hope in her eyes. "Oh, Gav, so insistent." She runs her fingers through my hair one more time. "I should get to bed. I'll see you in the morning." She pushes her chair back, causing my hands to fall away. I settle on my knees and watch her go. I wasn't positive that my feelings for her were love, but after today, after just a small moment of time where she was mine, pretending or not, I know it's love. I more than like her. I'm in love with her.

CHAPTER 10

I TOSSED AND TURNED ALL night. Sleep was not my friend as I replayed every minute of our day together, and then last night. I wanted to fall into his arms and let whatever happens, happen. I wanted to curl up in his arms and just… be. Instead, I pushed him away and retreated to my room.

We both admitted things we've never shared before. Made confessions that had my heart skipping a beat. He was right, though. We have so much in common, and if I allow myself to, I can see it… *us* together. It's clear in my mind, but so are the memories of growing up and watching my mother sacrifice for me. One incident in particular stands out. I had a school Christmas play and was required to wear dress shoes. I didn't have dress shoes. It was a luxury that we couldn't afford. Mom's shoes she wore to work were ragged with a hole in one toe. It was hard to tell how old they were. She needed them desperately and had been saving here and there to get a pair. Instead, she used that money to buy me a pair of black dress shoes. I cried and begged her not to. I knew how badly she needed those shoes, but she wanted me to feel like the rest of my classmates, just that one time. Luckily, the school provided a costume. I was a candy cane. All I was missing was the shoes.

I still have those shoes. They're tucked away in the original box in the back of my closet. I was maybe ten or eleven at the time and have held on to them all these years. She gave up so much for me to have them. It was a shame to just throw them away. I never wore them again after that day. There was no reason to. We didn't go anywhere fancy, not even church. Mom worked too much. We both did once I was of age.

Glancing at the clock, I see it's a little after ten. We planned to leave at noon, to catch a few more bands. Shattered Heart takes the stage at nine, but there's so much to see. The other bands, all the food booths, the local beers, the craft and retail tables that are set up. I was excited for all of it, I still am, but I'm worried about Gavin. Actually, I'm worried about me. Will I be able to hold strong and keep my head focused on the bigger picture?

Instead of dwelling any longer, I climb out of bed and head to the shower. I pick out a pair of white jean shorts that are frayed on the ends, and a pink tank top with a paisley pattern that flows, because it's forecast to be a hot day. I slide my feet into some brown sandals and call it good.

"Hey," Gavin greets me. "I was thinking since we both slept so late we could just grab lunch at the festival?"

"You're not going to hear any complaints from me." I offer him a smile that he returns. I take in a slow, calming breath. We can do this. We can know what we know, remember last night, and still be professional. We've got this.

"I didn't think so." He chuckles. "I'm ready when you are."

"I'm good. Just need to grab my bag." I gather my crossbody, slide my phone inside, and turn to face him. "Let's do this."

He holds out his hand and then lets it drop at his side. His face falls, but he recovers quickly. "After you," he says, walking to our door and holding it open for me.

I choose to ignore the tension in the elevator. It's different than yesterday, and I don't want to think about it. So I pretend it's not there. Somehow, we manage to make it all the way to the lobby without stopping. That's how it happened yesterday, too. There have to be hundreds of guests at this hotel with the festival, yet we never seem to be interrupted. I choose to ignore that, too. It's not a sign; at least, that's what I'm opting to believe. When the doors slide open, we both rush out, and I swear I can hear him inhale the same time as I do.

"I thought we could get a cab today. I'm sure there will be plenty of local brews for us to try."

"I was actually going to suggest that. It's no fun to try them alone."

"You're never alone with me," he says before asking the front desk to call us a cab. "I should have called ahead. I wasn't thinking," he confesses.

I don't ask what was on his mind. I don't need to. "So, any other bands on our radar?"

"Not specifically, but you know we're always looking. Let me know if one stands out to you."

"We pretty much have the same tastes," I say without thinking. His eyes heat as he looks at me.

"Yeah," he agrees. I can see the want there, and it's so damn hard to turn away from it.

The cab ride is filled with chatter from the driver. He's a huge Soul Serenade fan and talks Gavin's ear off all the way to the festival. He badgers him with questions about news of making a new album and fist bumps him on his shoulder for being the last to holdout on marriage. I listen halfheartedly, but the question has me sitting up and taking note. So does his answer. It could be because he presses his leg into mine when he says, "Nah, man. I'm not holding out. Just waiting for her to realize she's the only one I want."

Thankfully, the cab pulls up outside the festival entrance. "Before you go, can I get your autograph?" he asks.

I busy myself with pulling a sharpie from my bag and passing it to Gavin. I've learned over the years to always keep a couple handy. The guys can't go anywhere without someone asking them for an autograph. Once I hand it to him, I reach for my door handle to climb out and wait for him, but he stops me with his hand on my knee.

"Wait for me." Quickly, he scribbles his name on the guy's hat and a piece of paper, then gives me a nod to climb out. Instead of using his door, he follows me out of mine. That's Gav. Hell, that's all four of the Soul Serenade crew. They don't fit the usual rocker "I don't have a care in the world" vibe. I don't have to ask him why he had me wait. I know why.

"You're a beautiful woman in a crowd of drunk, rowdy, and horny men. Stay close," he says, confirming what I already knew.

"You worry too much," I tell him. He gives me a "don't give me that shit" look, and I laugh. "Right, where should we start?" With the question I dismiss that part of our conversation.

"Let's get you fed," he says. His hand goes to the small of my back to guide me through the crowd. He's done this hundreds of times, but today it feels different. It's an intimate act, at least in my eyes, but today it's as if he's reaching inside and grabbing a hold of my heart.

It's going to be a long day.

Gavin leads us to a french fry booth and I turn to grin at him. "It's like you read my mind."

"I know you, Cass." His hot breath whispers against my ear.

My body shivers. It's a good ninety degrees out, so there's no way to pass it off on the weather. Gavin moves in behind me, his hands on my hips as we wait in line. To anyone watching, we're together. My heart pleads with me, while my head reminds me there's too much at stake.

Maybe I should start looking for another job?

If I can earn a salary close to what I'm making now, I could still afford to keep Mom in the assisted-living facility and keep my apartment. Then I could listen to my heart. Then I could lean into him without worry that it will lead to more than what we could ever have. I'd hate to leave the label as I love the guys, their wives, and kids, and I love what I do, but... Gavin.

CHAPTER 11

GAVIN

T HOSE LITTLE WHITE SHORTS ARE going to be the death of me. If not
them, then it will be all these motherfuckers I start throwing hands
with because they can't keep their eyes off her. Not that I blame them,
but fuck me. I want to pull her close, capture her mouth with mine, let
them know she's with me. Because she is. She's mine. She knows it and
I know it. She just won't admit it. Not yet.

"I like this sound," she says over the noise of the crowd and points
to the stage. "I say we get a closer look."

I nod. I was thinking the same thing but chose to stay back, out of
the masses. Not because it bothers me, but I want her close and was
trying to respect her boundaries. However, she's asked, and I never want
to disappoint her. Lacing her fingers through mine, I lead us into the
crowd and closer to the stage. At first, her hand is loose in mine, but as
we become engulfed by the crowd, her hold tightens. I stop about five
rows back from the stage and guide her to stand in front of me. I wrap
my arms around her waist and pull her back against my chest. "I need
you safe and this is a rowdy bunch," I whisper in her ear. She
immediately relaxes into me, accepting my reasoning. She's a smart girl.
She's also a tiny thing, and this crowd would swallow her. Not on my
watch. I try to focus on the band, but I know I don't have to. They're

not who we're here to see, so instead, I focus on the feel of her in my arms again. How it feels to be holding her close. Satisfaction thrums through me that those around us know from how my arms are locked tightly around her, that she's off limits.

Cassidy pulls her cell phone out of her purse and holds it up in the air recording them. I agree this song has a good beat and the vocals are on point. The song ends and she places her phone back in her bag. When a ballad comes through the speakers, I feel it. The beat of the drums, the bass, and I imagine my fingers over the strings joining in. Cass sways a little to the beat, and once again, all my attention is on her. I match her rhythm as the lead singer croons about the love of his life. I wish I could tell her that she's mine. She's not ready to hear it yet. We'll get there.

The song ends and another begins. Cassidy turns to face me and I keep my arms locked around her. "Thirsty," she says, sticking her tongue out.

I smile down at her. She's so damn beautiful. "Stay close," I order. Reaching out, she places her hand in mine, and I lead us out of the thick of the crowd.

"Water or beer?" I ask once we stop where we can talk without yelling.

"Beer." She grins. "There are too many to sample."

"How about we try that stout?" I point to a booth just a few feet away.

"Perfect."

Her hand still in mine, we walk to the booth, and I order us both a beer. "Not bad," I say after taking a drink.

"Meh, I've had better."

She loves her beers. We spend the next several hours walking to all the booths. We don't buy anything, but she loves to look and I love to be by her side, so we're both content. By the time Shattered Heart takes the stage, we've sampled several of the food booths, and about six new beers. The final pale ale we tried is the one we've stuck with all afternoon and into the evening.

"Shattered Heart goes on in fifteen minutes. We should head that way," she says, looking at her watch.

"We need to be close for this one."

"Do you want to go backstage?"

"No, we have an open invitation, but I want to witness them from the crowd. See what kind of show they put on."

"Good idea. I'll record them so the guys can see it as well."

Tossing our empty cups from our most recent beer, I reach for her hand. She takes mine as if it's second nature and we make our way through the crowd once again. No other bands have really caught our eye, or should I say ear after that first one. I get us close, about five rows back just like before. This time, she walks in front of me without me guiding her. Most of these people have been here all day and have been drinking for hours. She knows to stay close.

They're not the only ones who've been drinking all day. Although I slowed down to make sure I would be coherent when Shattered Heart took the stage, I'd say we're both buzzed, but not so much that we don't know what's going on and can't make a decision about if the band is indeed what we're looking for.

My arms are wrapped around her as we sway to the beat. I've held her hand all afternoon. I expected her to pull away, but she didn't so I kept reaching for her. I'll always reach for her.

"HELLOOO, Missouri!" the lead singer shouts as the band takes their place on stage. "We're Shattered Heart." The crowd goes wild. This is the loudest I've heard them all day.

"They seem to be a crowd favorite," I whisper in her ear.

"I can see why." She giggles.

"Oh, yeah? Care to enlighten me?" I ask, nipping at her ear. I know exactly what she's going to say. I'm a man, but I'm not blind. I know when another dude has what the ladies love. The lead singer, Brian, is covered in ink, has dark spiky hair, his arms are huge, and from the tightness of his T-shirt, he's in good shape. I can hear the women sending catcalls his way.

"He's hot," she says over her shoulder, her lips almost touching mine.

"Yeah? Does he turn you on? Does he make you wet?" I ask, moving one hand to the waistband of her white shorts that have been driving me crazy all fucking day. I've never talked to her like this, but fuck me, she's got me worked up and talking about another man, she knows what she's doing.

"Gavin," she breathes. If my face were not buried in her neck, I would have missed it.

"What, baby?" I run my finger under the waistline of her shorts. "Tell me," I urge her.

"N-no," she stammers.

I stop moving my hand. "Okay," I whisper, defeated. I move to pull my finger from her waistband, trying to decide if I should release my hold on her, too. I can't quite bring myself to do it.

"Stop." She rests her hand over mine. Turning in my arms, she places her hands on my cheeks. I bend down so I can hear her. "No, he doesn't turn me on. Not the way you do."

Her eyes tell me everything I need to know. They're filled with desire and longing. Leaning in just a little further, I capture her lips with mine. She doesn't even hesitate as she nips at my lips. Her hands move from my face to grip my shirt. Her grip is strong as she pulls us closer. My hands clamp tight around her waist, holding her to my chest. My dick, which is hard as steel, presses against her. And when her tongue tangles with mine, she moans.

I need to get a hold of the situation before I fuck her right here, right now. Crowd be damned. Slowly, I pull away, kissing her softly on the lips, trailing my mouth toward her ear. "We have to slow down, Cass. I'm two seconds from taking you here." She gasps, and I know that's the moment reality of where we are comes crashing into her. She buries her head in my chest, and I wrap my arms around her, holding her close. As if the universe is cheering us on, Shattered Heart begins one of their ballads. I don't let her go. Instead, we sway to the beat as I try to focus on the band. That's why I'm here after all. Not to seduce my girl. Then again, if we leave here with her admitting that she's mine, fuck the band. The guys will understand. It's all in the name of love, right?

The song ends and the next one begins, this one faster, more upbeat. Cass doesn't pull away, but she stops swaying to the beat. She's holding on tightly, and no way am I letting her go. Not when I finally have her where I want her. I run my hands up and down her back, just enjoying the feel of her in my arms. We stay this way for four more songs before she pulls away and looks up at me. It's now dark and we only have the lights from the stage and the surrounding booths, but I can imagine her sapphire eyes. I don't need to see them.

Standing on her tiptoes, she presses a tender kiss to my lips. "I need to record them," she says before turning and pulling out her phone. My hands rest on her hips. She's given me no indication that she no longer wants me to touch her, so I'm not stopping.

As soon as the first chord is played, the crowd goes crazy. Our little circle gets even smaller as people crowd around us, vying to get closer to the stage, closer to the action. I wrap my arms back around her waist, protecting her from the madness. Surrounded by chaos, my world is still as she rests her head against my shoulder, holding her cell phone in the air and recording the entire song.

One song bleeds into another, while she records and I hold her tight. No longer able to resist temptation, I slide my hand under her shirt and rest it on her belly. She lowers her phone, and I bury my face in her neck, kissing her heated skin. My lips trail up to her ear. "I can't stop touching you," I confess. Her answer is to tilt her head, giving me better access. I take it, not questioning what's changed her mind, why she's giving in. My lips devour her neck. Licking. Biting. Sucking. Kissing.

"How you all doing tonight?" The lead singer addresses the crowd.

"Fucking fantastic," I whisper in her ear, causing her to laugh.

"This next one is new. We've got some special friends out there in the crowd tonight, and we wanted to show them what Shattered Heart is all about." The crowd roars. "This one, it's all about making love." He laughs. "They tell me that's the right way to talk about fucking on stage," he admits, and the roar of the crowd is thunderous.

The song starts out slow and smooth. The beat of the drum and the bass guitar are in perfect harmony. Closing my eyes, I imagine making love to Cass with this in the background. She turns in my arms and wraps one arm around my waist, the other rests on my chest. I slip my hand back under her shirt, because the feel of her skin against my fingers is… life altering. She rests her head against me as she slides her hand lower until hers, too, is under my shirt. Only she stops once she reaches the waistband of my jeans. Her finger slides underneath, which causes her to brush the tip of my cock.

She looks up, eyes wide.

"That's all you," I say, my lips next to her ear.

She does it again.

And again.

She's driving me fucking wild. Looking around at the crowd, I know we can't do this here. Not with her. She's better than that. I've been recognized several times today. Thankfully, it's been calm, a few autographs, but this... I don't want her on the front of some dirty tabloid. I need to find a spot and find it now. "Come with me," I whisper. I make sure I have a tight grip on her hand and guide her through the crowd. Looking at my watch, I know the band will be on stage for at least another hour. Time to cash in on that backstage offer.

I lead us to the security gate, and the guy recognizes me automatically. "Gavin McIntosh, it's a pleasure to meet you." He holds out his hand for me to shake.

"You too," I reply, not bothering to get his name. It doesn't matter. All that matters in this moment is him leading me backstage to a private room.

"We're trying to get away from the madness for a while. You think there's a room back there we can chill in until the set is over?"

"Yeah, man. We have one all set up for the meeting after. Follow me," he says. He calls over another guard. They share a few words and then we're walking. He stops outside of a trailer and pulls keys from his pocket. "This is all set up for later. Help yourselves to drinks and food. The band will be here after their set."

"Thanks." I hold my hand out for him and we shake. Breaking away, I lead Cass into the trailer, shutting the door and locking it behind us. "Come here," I say into the darkness. I don't bother turning on the lights. I don't want anyone to see into the windows and if the lights stay off, they don't know we're in here. More privacy.

Cassidy steps into me and places her hand on the waistband of my jeans. I stand still, letting her take the lead. She doesn't make me wait long when I feel her unbutton my jeans and slide the zipper down.

"Baby, are you sure about this?" I ask her. She doesn't answer me, not with words. She does reach under the waistband of my boxer briefs and palm my cock though. That's answer enough. My hands are on her in an instant. I have her shorts unbuttoned and slid past her hips in no time. She kicks them to the side. I follow her lead and slide my hand inside her silk panties. "So wet." I breathe the words against her neck. "Fuck, Cass." Running my fingers through her folds, she shudders, and her grip on my cock strengthens.

I suck on her neck, not giving a fuck if I mark her. I want every-fucking-one to know she's mine. My fingers are coated with her, but it's not enough. I want more. Carefully, I slide one finger inside and she moans.

"Talk to me, Cass."

"More," she breathes.

Pulling out, I slowly add another. Leisurely, I pump my fingers in and out of her, as if I have all the time in the world. However, my heart is thundering, and with her soft hand wrapped around my cock, I feel like I could lose my shit at any second.

Sliding my hand around the back of her neck, I pull her into a kiss. Her hands pump faster, matching the rhythm of my fingers that are nestled inside of her. In and out, up and down, we chase our release. Her walls tighten around my fingers, and I know she's close. "Give it to me," I say against her lips. "I want to feel you fall apart." She makes a sound that comes from deep in the back of her throat. Her hand tightens on my shaft, while the other lets go and grabs my arm, her nails digging into the skin.

"Gavin." She moans my name as she coats my hand. I close my eyes and let go, spilling into hers. I'm breathing like I just ran a fucking marathon; my body feels as though it did. My legs are like wet noodles, but I'm the most relaxed I've felt in months. Lifting her into my arms, she instinctively wraps her legs around my waist, and I carry her to one of the chairs. Sitting with her in my lap, wrapped around me. Her pussy and all its wetness from her releases press against my cock.

Spotting a pile of napkins in the soft glow of light through the windows, I reach for them and hand a few to her. "For your hands," I murmur.

Lifting her head from my shoulder, she takes the offered napkins and cleans off her hands the best she can. When her eyes catch mine, I place my fingers in my mouth and taste her for the first time. Her eyes heat as she watches my tongue trace over both digits. Pulling my fingers from my mouth, I take my napkins and clean her up as best as I can.

"What was that?" she asks softly.

"That, sweetheart, was months of wanting each other and denying what we know is right. That's you and me, Cass. We're right." I lift her palm to my lips and place a soft kiss in the center. Outside the crowd roars, reminding us where we are. "As bad as I hate to say this, we need to get dressed." I kiss her one more time before she climbs off my lap to find her clothes.

As I'm sliding my jeans back up my thighs, I can't help but hope this is going to be the beginning of us.

CHAPTER 12

W E'RE BARELY DRESSED AND HAVE the lights turned on when we hear a commotion outside the trailer door. Gavin takes a seat at the table, the same one we were both just sitting on. He pulls the chair beside him out and motions for me to sit. As soon as my ass hits the cheap vinyl, the door swings open. The members of Shattered Heart come barreling in, still on a high from their show.

I brush my fingers through my hair, making sure it's all back in place. My heart is still beating double time from the adrenaline of my orgasm and the fact that any longer and we could have been caught.

"Gavin McIntosh, I'm a huge fan. Name's Brian, lead vocals." He offers Gavin his hand.

Gavin shakes his hand, then those of the three other band members as they introduce themselves and tell him how big of a fan they are of Soul Serenade.

"And who's this?" Brian asks, giving me a skeevy smile.

Seriously, it's creepy as hell. I lift my hand to introduce myself when Gavin puts his arm around me.

"She's mine."

Brian raises his hand in an "I'm backing off" motion, and the four of them take seats across the table from us. They begin to talk about tonight's set, and I know I should be paying attention, but all I can hear is Gavin and those two words, "She's mine." I wish more than anything that was true. We took things too far tonight. I let it happen. I know that. It's on me. He never would have gone that far had he not had my permission. Hell, I practically threw myself at him.

Shaking out of my thoughts, I try to focus on the conversation going on around me. It's hard with the feel of his hands all over me, and currently, his arm is thrown over my shoulders, and his fingers are lazily tracing invisible patterns. I should be able to handle it, but after what we just shared, my senses are on high alert.

"We were impressed," Gavin says, giving my shoulder a gentle squeeze. "How long have you all been together?" He asks questions and interacts as if he hasn't a care in the world. Maybe he doesn't. Maybe our tryst didn't rock his world like it did mine. Maybe he's changed his mind after all.

I jump when I feel his hot breath against my ear. "I can still feel you," he whispers, and I have to bite down on my cheek to keep from moaning. He moves his arm from my shoulders to rest on my bare thigh.

"What does your schedule look like the rest of the summer? I'd like to have you come back to Nashville and perform for the guys."

"Fuck yes!" Brian cheers.

Shattered Heart on stage has a great presence. Their sound's unique and their material is their own. All good points for the label. However, they need a little... refining. Some people skills. I would like to think they would attempt a little more professionalism considering who we are and why we're here. Then again, they're young, cocky rock stars on the verge of potentially signing a major deal with the number one rock band in the country's new label. All things considered, "fuck yes" is a pretty good response.

"You should hang out, drink a few," Eric, the lead guitarist, offers.

"Thank you, but we've been here all day. I think we're just going to head back to the hotel. We'll be in touch once we get back to the office next week to confirm details of your visit."

"You sure? We'd love to party with you," Brian says, never taking his eyes off me.

"We're sure," Gavin grits out, his voice hard. He stands and holds out his hand for me. I take it and stand as well. My legs are wobbly, but his arm around my waist holds me steady. Gavin walks toward the door of the trailer, then turns to face the guys.

"Your sound is good, your material better. I think Soul Records can take you to the next level." He stops as the guys smile and nod. "However, I would advise you to keep your eyes and your thoughts about my girl hidden. In fact, don't think about her at all. When you visit the label, the other wives will be there as well. I advise you to take this piece of advice to heart with all four of them." They spit and splutter, offering apologies, when really it was just Brian who made me feel uncomfortable. Gavin doesn't seem to want to hear it as he opens the door and leaves them and their apologies behind in the trailer.

"Ready to head to the hotel?" he asks.

"Yeah, it's been a long day."

He nods. Leaning in, he kisses my temple. "Yeah, it's been a long day, but one I'll never forget." His arm's already around my waist, so I do the same, wanting to hold on to him just a little longer. I'm exhausted, and my mind is racing a million miles a minute, but I'm not ready for this day to end. I'm not ready to go back to keeping him at arm's length. When we reach the gate, I rest against his chest as he pulls up his Uber app and orders us a car.

Gavin slides his phone back in his pocket and wraps both arms around me, holding me tight. "Let me say this," he says, his voice low and next to my ear. Controlled. I keep my head buried in his chest. "I want you, Cassidy. I want you with a need so deep, I don't ever see it going away. I've enjoyed every minute of today. To have you fall apart in my arms…." He swallows thickly. "I want you to be mine, Cass. For tonight, for tomorrow, for always."

Tears well in my eyes. I want it. Everything he just said, I want it, too. There's just too much at stake. It sounds like an excuse even to me, but all I have to do is think about Mom, to think about those shoes that are hidden away in the back of my closet. Mom made the sacrifice and so will I.

When the car shows up, Gavin opens the back door, allowing me to climb in first. He rattles off the information for our hotel and wraps his arm around me. I don't hesitate to snuggle into his chest. We have two more days before we leave town. I can't help but wonder how things are going to be in the light of day? After today, how can we go back to how we used to be?

The drive back to the hotel is short, and as we exit the car, I feel the tears start to build. Our day is over. Never again will I feel his hands roam over my body or the feel of his lips pressed against mine. It's tearing me up inside because even though I can't have him, he's all I want.

This time when we step into the elevator, there are several people who pile in with us. Gavin stands tall and strong behind me, holding me close to him. I don't know what will happen when we get to our room or how we handle this. My palms are sweating and my emotions are all over the place.

By the time the elevator doors open on our floor, it's just us. Hand on my hips, Gavin guides me out and to our suite. I remove the keycard from my purse and slide it into the lock. Slowly, I turn the handle and push the door open. Gavin, with his hands still on my hips, follows me. When the door closes, I wince. Hot tears behind my eyes threaten to fall. I don't want this day to end. I close my eyes to keep him from seeing everything that I'm feeling.

When his lips land on my neck, I swallow back my emotions. Tilting my head to the side, I give him better access. His lips are heaven, so much so a small moan falls from my lips.

With slight pressure on my hips, he turns me to face him. Leaving one hand around my waist, the other tucks an errant curl behind my ear. "So, beautiful," he whispers, and I offer him a shy smile, slowly opening my eyes. He's watching me. His blue eyes are intense as they show his need for me in this moment.

He leans in, watching me closely, waiting for me to stop him. I won't. Not tonight. A little further and his mouth is closing in on mine. I help him out by wrapping my hands around the back of his neck, running my fingers through his hair. And then I pull him the rest of the way to me.

He nips at my lips, then traces them with his tongue, soothing the pain. Needing more of him, more of everything, I slide my tongue past his lips, taking control of the kiss. He lets out a guttural moan. His hands fall to my ass and he lifts me. Instinctively, I wrap my legs around his waist. Then we're moving. In a few long strides, Gavin has my back pressed against the wall.

It was silly of me to think I would be in control. Gavin takes charge, his tongue caressing mine while his hands knead my ass cheeks. I tighten my legs around his waist, pressing my core against his erection.

"You want my cock?" he asks, breathless against my neck.

"Mmmm." I can't seem to form words with his hands and mouth on me.

"I need your words, Cass," he says, trailing kisses along my neck. "I need to hear you say it, baby," he whispers in my ear.

"Y-yes," I manage to say, tilting my head back to rest against the wall.

"How drunk are you?"

I shake my head. "Not."

"Look at me," he insists. "Tell me. Let me see your eyes." My gaze connects with his. "You want this?"

"I want you. I'm buzzed but not enough to not know what I'm saying." Untangling my hands from his hair, I cup his face in my hands. "I want you and your cock." I grin.

He kisses me hard before stepping away from the wall and moving us, me still in his arms, still wrapped tightly around him. He heads toward his room.

Once inside, he kisses me one more time before I unwrap my legs from around his waist as he sets me back on my feet. "Arms up," he says, reaching for the hem of my shirt. I do as he asks, and he lifts my shirt over my head, dropping it to the floor. I reach for his but don't have to ask as he follows my lead and lifts his arms in the air, already knowing what I want. Dropping his shirt to the floor with mine, I make quick work of sliding my shorts down my legs, kicking them to the side.

"Fuck me, you're gorgeous." He reaches out and traces the swell of my breasts secured in my black lace bra with the tip of his index finger.

"You're wearing too many clothes, Gav," I whisper, reaching for the button on his jeans.

Without saying a word, he strips out of his jeans and boxer briefs at the same time, letting them pool at his feet. Bending over, he digs in his pocket for a condom. When he stands up to his full height, he has it between his fingers and is wearing a sly grin. "Now who's wearing too many clothes?" He leans over and trails his lips up my stomach.

"What are you going to do about it?" I ask more boldly. I've never been this outspoken during sex. There's just something about Gavin that makes me feel like I can be brave, be me.

His lips move to the waistband of my silk panties. With his teeth, he tugs them away from my skin. "These need to go," he says, and I lift my hips helping him. With deft fingers, my panties are discarded. "Sit up," he instructs, and I do, resting my hands on his bare shoulders. His lips mold with mine in a slow, sensual kiss, while his fingers unclasp my bra. Breaking away from our kiss, he slides the straps down each shoulder before tossing it over his shoulder. "Never thought I'd get the chance to see you like this," he confesses.

"You thought about it?" I ask him, despite already knowing the answer. I'm nervous and chatty, and truth be told, I want the answer reaffirmed. I want to know if he's put as much mental effort into what we could be as I have.

"Every fucking day since the day I met you," he assures me. "I don't know where to start first."

Reaching out, I wrap my hands around his length. "I say we start with this."

"So bold," he whispers. "Tell me what you want."

"This," I stroke him, "inside of me."

"Slide back." He motions for me to slide back on the bed. He's peering down at me with so much heat and... affection in his gaze. I can't look away. Instead, I do as he asks and scoot back, resting my head on the pillow. Gavin follows after me, resting back on his knees between my legs. "I'll give you what you want, but I need you to know that before this night is through, my lips will have touched every inch of your skin. My tongue will know the curves of your body, and my hands will be branded with your touch."

"Please," I beg. I want that. All of it. Everything he said and more. I want all of it and I want it now. Somewhere in the back of my mind, I know I'm crossing the line that's going to be impossible to step back over, but in this moment, with him stroking his hard cock and looming over me, I can't seem to find it in me to care. I'll deal with the fallout when it comes. Right now, he's all I can see. He's all I need.

I don't take my eyes off him as he rolls the condom down his hard length. He strokes himself leisurely, teasing me. "Say it again, Cassidy. Tell me this is what you want."

"This is what I want," I repeat the words.

As if I'm watching him in slow motion, he moves forward, resting his elbows on either side of my head. "Hey." He smiles and kisses my lips quickly. I open for him, and greedily suck on his tongue. It's then that he slides inside me. "I don't want to hurt you," he says against my lips as he slowly pushes inside one torturously slow inch at a time.

I wrap my legs around his waist and lock my feet at his back, using pressure to pull him into me. "Faster," I plead, closing my eyes and letting the feeling of him inside me take over.

"I can't," he grits out. "I can't go faster, Cass." I open my eyes to see him staring down at me. "I don't know when I'm going to be here again, inside of you." Resting his weight on one arm, the free hand cups my cheek. "I want to feel it all, memorize it all."

"We can do it again," I say, trying to get my way, even though the truth of his words hurt my heart. I think he sees right through me.

"Oh, baby." He chuckles. "I hope so," he says, pushing one more time to be fully seated inside of me.

I wait, hoping he'll start to move, and he does, but it's not the fast, hectic fucking that I expect from him. No. This is slow and deliberate. He's not just fucking me. He's making love to me. I expected hard, fast, and frantic. What he's giving me is slow, sweet, gentle, and I know without a doubt I'll never be the same. I had thought I could look back on this night with a fondness of sharing my body with him, a round of hot sweaty sex that we've been dancing around of months. This is not what I expected. His soul is speaking to mine, insistent as ever… that no man could ever make me feel as I do in this moment.

"So good," he whispers, rocking his hips.

"Gavin." His name is a plea on my lips, but I don't even know what I'm asking for. For more of him? For him to be mine? It's all things I want, things I know I can have if I would just let myself take the chance. It's risky, and the stakes are high, but being consumed with him, to feel him inside me like this, it makes me wonder if this risk might just be worth it.

Gavin rolls his hips, and I grip his back, my nails digging into the skin. "So deep," he murmurs, kissing my lips, my eyes, my nose, and my cheeks. His lips are gentle and everywhere. "My Cass," he says before burying his face in my neck.

My heart skips a beat in my chest. His words have tears welling in my eyes. I bite down on my bottom lip and force them back. I want to be his and for him to be mine. If only things were different. I feel him everywhere. He's branded my skin. And him inside of me... nothing has ever felt this way, and I'm sure never will again. Not unless it's with Gavin.

"Fuck. I can't get enough of you," he says, nipping at my ear.

"I-I'm close." I tighten my grip on his back. My nails are digging deep, but I can't seem to help it. I need him close, need to be tethered to him.

"Let me feel you, Cassidy. Let me feel you let go with my cock inside of you."

His words push me over the edge. My legs squeeze him, my nails dig deeper, and all I can do is hold on for the ride as he finally quickens his pace and my orgasm washes over me.

"Fuck, Cass," he says as his eyes close and a deep rumble falls from his lips. He jerks inside of me a few more times before he stills and rests his head on my shoulder.

Realizing that I still have a death grip on him, I let my legs fall to the bed and instead of digging into his back, I stroke him with soft caresses while waiting for his next move. We just crossed over that invisible line and awkwardness is sure to set I in. I'm not sure how I'm supposed to act? Can I pretend I don't love him? Will I be able to pretend like this night was nothing more than a roll in the sheets? Will I be able to hide behind the pain of knowing I'll never feel this way again?

CHAPTER 13

GAVIN

I SUCK IN AIR, TRYING to get my breathing under control. I'm wrecked, completely and totally wrecked, and I know without a doubt sex will never be the same for me. Not unless it's with Cass. Fuck, she's incredible. Every delectable inch of her is perfect. Her legs fall open and her hands trace up and down my back. I know I need to pull away and say something. I'm also man enough to admit that lifting my head and facing her scares the hell out of me. I know her. She's already regretting letting us cross that invisible divide. I don't want to hear her tell me that what we just shared was a mistake. We both know better.

"You okay?" she asks, her voice quiet.

Reluctantly, I lift my head and let my softening cock slide out of her. "Yeah. I'll be right back." I roll out of bed and rush to the bathroom to get rid of the condom. I'm not even sure I made the trash can, ready to get back to her before she decides to escape to her own room. I slide in beside her and pull the cover up over us. "Come here." I hold my arms open, asking her to come to me.

I breathe a little easier when she does. "You're warm," she says, snuggling into my side.

"You cold?"

INSISTENT

"No, but I'm not going to pass up your warmth either," she admits.

I hold her in my arms as a hundred words run through my mind. Things I should say, things I want to say, and things I know she doesn't want to hear. I don't know where to start, so I just start talking and let my brain decide for me. "Today, being with you, holding you close, just spending the day with you… all of it was incredible. Then tonight, first at the festival and now here…." I shake my head. "I get paid to write songs and perform them, but I can't seem to find words to explain to you what I'm feeling."

"Try," she whispers.

Not what I was expecting. I expected her to tell me it was a mistake. That we knew better. "Happy, deliriously happy. Content, sated." I lean in and kiss her. "And dare I say loved. Getting to touch you like this after all this time, to feel your heat around me, the way we came together." I pause, collecting my thoughts. "We're good together, Cassidy. You're all I see. All I want. I can't stop thinking about you, and I can only imagine after what we've shared today that's only going to increase tenfold. I give you my word that things won't change and if for some reason you decide to kick my ass to the curb…" I kiss her again, because, I can't not. "…if that happens, I'll fight you on it. I will not give you up without a fight. But at the end of the day, if being with me is no longer what you want, I promise you that your job is safe, that you have a home at Soul Records as long as you want it. I can put it in writing if you want," I add.

She's quiet for the longest time. I don't say another word, fearful of what her reply is going to be. Instead, I hold her close, running my fingers through her curls, waiting for her to process what I said. What I didn't say was that I can't ever see myself not wanting her. Not wanting to feel her hand in mine, or the press of her lips against my skin, or the feel of her heat. I know without a doubt she's it for me. *The* one. I know Cass well enough that she's not ready to hear that just yet. Baby steps.

Her hand rests on my chest, right over my heart and when she starts to speak, I hold my breath waiting to hear what she's going to say.

"Everything has changed, yet nothing has changed," she says cryptically. I stay quiet, releasing the breath I was holding, waiting for her to gather her thoughts. "Everything has changed, because now I know what it's like to be with you, to have all of your attention and your affection. To be one with you," she says shyly. "I know what I've been

64

missing." Her fingers pause from tracing circles on my chest. They rest over my heart. "Flip the coin and nothing has changed. I'm still responsible for my mom's care. I'm still willing to sacrifice just as she did to ensure she's well taken care of. I'm at a crossroads, Gavin, and I don't know what to do." Although I hate that it's not what I want to hear, I appreciate her honesty. I need it to guide me in my pursuit to show her we can have it both ways. We can have it all. When she lifts her head from my chest, I see tears welling in her eyes. "I wish—" She swallows hard. "—I wish there was an easy answer. I wish I could have it both ways, but the fear of losing my means to provide for her is too strong. It was just us, Gavin, just me and my mom against the world. She's all I have, and no way can I jeopardize that. Hell, I probably already have."

"Trust me," I say before kissing the corner of her mouth.

"It's not that I don't trust you, Gavin. It's that I don't trust me getting lost in you. It's not if I do, it's when I do. If I'm honest with myself, I'm halfway there. I think about you all the time. I often wonder what it would be like to stop fighting this. I just can't do it."

"So, what does that mean?" I ask, even though I know the answer.

"That means we have a couple of days. We've already broken the rules and crossed the professional lines. We have the rest of our time here, and when we get back home, we go back to being Cassidy and Gavin. Boss and employee. Friends, if you'll still have me."

I squeeze her to me, not knowing what to say. I want to say fuck no. No way is just the next two days enough for me, but then I think about the alternative. She goes to her room, and I stay here in mine with the smell of her on my sheets. I want all of her, but I'm a starving man and she's my salvation. I'll take her any way that I can get her.

"I want you, Cass. The thought of this week, two fucking days being all I get with you feels like steel in the pit of my stomach. But the thought of never touching you again, even for those two days, that's worse. So much worse." Kissing her temple, I mull it over one more time before giving her my answer. "I'll take as little or as much of you as you're willing to give me. Whether that's here or back at home. You're calling the shots here, Cass."

Her head lifts and those sapphire eyes of hers look hopeful. "Then we have two days." Her hand cups my cheek. "Let's make the most of them, Gav."

INSISTENT

I nod, still unsure of my decision. My only hope is that the next two days will cement what we are when we're together: nothing short of spectacular. Then maybe she'll realize two days will never be enough. Here's to hoping things go my way. If not, well, I just might have to make them. I'm not giving her up without a fight, whether it's two days or two years. It hits me that I've lied to her. However, when it comes to matters of the heart, you can't really plan. That's my saving grace. At least I hope it will be when she realizes that I never intended to end things here.

CHAPTER 14

Cassidy

THE MORNING SUN CREEPS IN through the windows of our suite. I've been up for a while just thinking. Gavin's arms are locked around me, so moving is out of the question. Not that I would want to. We didn't leave the room yesterday, at all. He declared that if he only got to have me for two days, we were going to make the best of it. I imagined he wanted sex all day, but it was the opposite. I mean, yeah, we had sex—great, amazing, toe-curling sex—but it was more than that. We kissed for hours, and we took a bath in the ridiculously huge tub in his room. We watched movies and ordered tons of room service. I can't remember a day where I had been so content and happy. We fell into bed last night and Gavin made love to me. Slower than any of the times before, kissing every inch of my skin, branding me with his five o'clock shadow. I'll never be the same, and I'm good with that. What is it they say, *it's better to have loved and lived than to have never loved at all?* We're making memories that I will forever hold near and dear to my heart.

Just like Gavin, who will always be near and dear to my heart. At this point he owns it, but I can't tell him that. Not if I want him to keep to our agreement and have things go back to the way they were before this trip. I'm not convinced they will anyway. It's wishful thinking. Not to mention he gave in way too quickly. I have a feeling I'm going to have a fight on my hands when we get back, but if I'm anything, it's stubborn. I know what I need to do. It's the sacrifice I have to make.

"Morning, beautiful," Gavin says, kissing my bare shoulder.

"Morning."

"How long have you been awake?"

"Not long. You wore me out," I tease.

He slides his hand over my breast, cupping it gently. "What do you want to do today?" he asks. His voice is husky and I know what he's thinking.

"You mean I have a choice? You're not holding me captive?"

"I can. Is that what you want?"

"I want you," I say, rolling over to face him.

"You have me, baby. Any way you want me, you have me," he says, moving my mass of curls out of my eyes.

"What do you want to do?"

"I don't care as long as I get to touch you and kiss you whenever I want."

"I kinda just want to stay in."

"Nothing else in St. Louis you want to see? More of the festival?"

"No. I just want this time with you."

He leans in and kisses me—soft, slow, sweet, and everything I've come to learn is exactly Gavin. "That's what my girl wants, that's what she gets." He smiles.

My girl. Oh, how I wish I could be. "So, I say we order room service and shower. Maybe we'll go down to the pool for a while or something, but I would rather just be here with you. Limit the distractions as much as possible."

"That all sounds good, babe, but there's something that we need to do first," he says, running his hands up my bare thighs.

"Oh, yeah? What's that?"

"I have to have you." He leans in for a kiss.

"You just had me." I look over his shoulder at the alarm clock on the nightstand. "Less than four hours ago." I chuckle.

"I know, it's too damn long."

"We need a shower."

"Shower sex it is," he says, rolling out of bed. He stalks butt-naked to my side of the bed, throws the covers back, and scoops me up in his arms. "Great idea." He smirks.

"I can walk you know," I remind him.

"Yeah, but then your sexy body wouldn't be nestled against me. Bigger picture, Cass. Look at the bigger picture." He laughs, setting me down on the cold counter. I yelp at the contact. "Don't worry, I'll warm you up." He kisses me quickly before turning to start the water in the shower.

I watch him as he tests the water, waiting for it to warm. This week has taught me so much. Things like he forever puts me first, no matter if it's ordering lunch or in the bedroom. I've also learned my initial assumption about him was correct—he's more than his job, not just a rock star looking to get laid any chance he can get. The Soul Serenade guys are a rare breed when they fall. For me, I'm the lucky one who gets his attention and affection. It breaks my heart that it will be so short-lived. This is our last day together. The last night that I will fall asleep in his arms and wake up the same way. I'm not looking forward to life after St. Louis. There is still that nagging in the back of my mind that I could look for another job, then we could be together. It's a big step, but Gavin is worth it.

"Hey." His hands cup my face. "Where did you go?" he asks, watching me closely.

"Just thinking," I tell him honestly.

"Want to share?"

"Today is our last day and night together."

"Doesn't have to be." His eyes bore into mine.

"Gavin," I sigh. I knew this was how he would react.

"I'm just stating the obvious. This doesn't have to end, Cassidy. None of it. You can be mine in Nashville just like you're mine here. In fact, I'd prefer it." His eyes never waver as they convey every word he's saying.

"We're wasting water," I say, nodding toward the shower.

"It's not our water," he fires back. "Think about it, Cass. That's all I ask." He leans in and kisses my forehead.

"I have, Gavin. I've thought about it and the consequences of the fallout."

INSISTENT

"I promised you I won't go back on that."

"You did," I agree. "But you forgot one little detail. I don't think I could handle being with you day in and day out and see you move on. That would break me."

"But that's what you're asking me to do. To move on, without you. I don't want to do that."

"I get that. I do. However, it would be worse if I had you for weeks, months, years, and then had to watch it. I couldn't take it."

"That's an easy fix." He waits for me to ask, knowing I will.

"How's that?" I give in easily.

"You never leave me."

"Right," I scoff. "It wouldn't be me leaving."

"You're so sure I'm just going to toss you to the curb. What do I have to do to prove to you that you're mine? I want it that way until the end of fucking time, Cassidy. What do I need to do to prove that to you?"

"You can't." I shake my head, tired of the same conversation, even though I was expecting it. I feel like I'm living in a loop, arguing the same things, reminding him of all the reasons why, and it's exhausting. "I need to call and check on Mom. Go ahead and shower first." I don't think I can do this anymore. It's already so difficult. I move to hop off the counter, but his hands on my hips stop me.

"No. Don't go. Fuck, Cass. I get one more day, and I don't want to spend it fighting with you. Please don't go. I'll drop it."

"It's just bad timing, Gavin."

"Come on." He lifts me from the counter, and I allow him to guide me into the shower as he follows behind me.

Stepping under the spray, I tilt my head back, letting the water wash over me. When I raise my head and open my eyes, I see he's watching me. Without a word, he steps closer, his hands resting on my hips. Something I've noticed he loves to do. When his lips descend on mine, our earlier disagreement is forgotten. The fact that this is our last day to be… us is forgotten. His touch washes it all away. His kiss is deep, passionate. I know he's trying to say everything we just said and more. He wants me to give this a chance, and I just won't do it. I know it's *won't* and not *can't,* and I need to live up to that. I'm being stubborn, but those little black shoes in my closet help keep me that way.

70

Cupping my ass, he lifts me, and I wrap my legs around his waist. He steps forward until my back hits the cool tile of the shower wall. He deepens the kiss. We're all teeth and lips and tongue, and it's hot as hell. "I need to be inside of you," he whispers.

I rock my hips and tighten my legs at the same time, making him moan. "Hurry," I pant, turning my head, breaking our kiss, letting his lips trail down my neck.

"Fuck," he hisses as he thrusts his hips.

His hard cock is pressed tight against my stomach, which is not where I need it. "Yes, that's the plan." I rock against him again.

"No condom," he says, his hot breath against my ear.

"I'm clean. It's been… a while for me, and I'm protected. Couple of years."

He stops, stands to his full height, and stares down at me. "What are you saying, Cass?"

"I'm saying if you leave this shower without fucking me, I'm going to be pissed." I smile, going for coy.

"I'm clean and it's been… about the same time for me."

I scoff. "Come on, Gavin. Be honest with me."

His forehead presses to mine. "I promise you. The day I decided I wanted you was the day I gave it up, the random women. It's only you, Cass. It's been that way for a while now."

Holy shit! There is not a doubt in my mind that he's telling me the truth—Gavin is a straight shooter—but this is not what I was expecting. Sure, I've noticed that the women are not around, but I'm not with him twenty-four hours a day. I just assumed he was keeping it to himself. What do I do with this information? I can feel myself falling deeper, getting more attached to him, and I know without a doubt that it will destroy me when we leave here. Opening my eyes, I see his are still closed tightly as his forehead is still pressed to mine. "What are you waiting for?" I ask. Slowly he lifts his head. He seems to be struggling with the decision, so I start to backpedal. "I mean, we don't have to. You can—"

He places his fingers over my lips. "I need you to know that this only happens with you. It's a first for me and… it's only you, Cassidy. Only you," he says, reaching between us and fisting his cock. Hands on his shoulders, I lift as he positions himself at my entrance. Slowly, I slide down, feeling the sweet ache that only happens when he's inside of me take hold.

I'm reeling from his confession, my heart pleading to be his. Once he's in, he buries his face in my neck. I feel the rapid rise and fall of his chest against mine. His grip on my thighs is tight, almost painful, but I don't tell him. This moment is raw and pure, and no way am I ruining it. Instead, I run my fingers through his wet hair; the dark blond locks turn darker when wet.

With great precision, he pulls out and slowly pushes back in. "Fuck, Cass. I don't know how long I'm going to last," he admits.

"Then don't," I say, gripping his hair in my hands. "Don't last, don't hold back. I can take it, Gavin. I want all of you, everything that's running through your mind. Whatever it is that's making your chest heave, let me have it. All of it."

Again, he thrusts, this time a little faster. "Hot, wet, tight, and so fucking incredible. Like nothing before you." He's talking in choppy sentences, but I get the meaning.

"For me too," I agree. "Feels… different."

"Yeah," he breathes, thrusting faster.

"Don't hold back."

"Help me, baby. I need you there with me. I can't go without you."

Sliding my hand between us, I rub over my clit and shudder, already feeling my orgasm building deep in my core. Gavin thrusts, harder and harder until it's all I can do to hold on. My hand drops as the overwhelming sensation builds higher and higher. My hands dig into his shoulders, holding on for the ride. "Yes," I moan, leaning my head against the shower wall.

"Cass, baby, I'm gonna come," he grunts, never breaking his rhythm, thrusting in and out, in and out, over and over, fast, rapid, and oh so fucking good.

"Gavin!" I shout his name as what feels like an electrical current of pure bliss rolls through my body. He follows after me, my name on his lips, his head buried in my neck. His grip on my thighs remains strong as he holds me to him.

When he lifts his head, his lips crash with mine. It's slow and sloppy, sensual and perfect. "I—" He shakes his head. "I imagined that with you, more times that I care to admit." His eyes soften. "My imagination didn't prepare me for the feeling of utter completeness while being inside of you with nothing between us."

"Better?" I ask.

He chuckles. "Better is an understatement. Life altering comes to mind." He grins. Carefully, he sets me on the shower floor. He drops to his knees and turns me, running his lips up the back of my thighs, kissing the marks where his fingers were digging in.

Looking down at him, I watch the rivulets of water run over his face while his hair covers his eyes as he worships me. At least that's what it feels like. That I'm cherished, and dare I say loved? I know my heart beats for him. I just wish I could tell him that. "I'm fine," I tell him when he looks up at me.

"I'm so sorry, Cass. I got carried away."

"No." I pull on his arms to get him to stand up. "You lost control. We both did. I did that to you, that's… empowering that I can bring a man like you to the brink of losing your control."

"A man like me?" he asks, pulling me into him, wrapping his arms around my waist.

"Yeah. You're no stranger to women and could have anyone you want. To know I'm the one you chose to experience that with… I like it." I shrug.

"Only you," he says, kissing my lips. "Now, let's get you washed off. We have room service to order, and you're pruning." He brings my water-wrinkled fingers to his lips for a kiss.

CHAPTER 15

GAVIN

M Y GRIP ON HER HAND is firm, and I don't want to let go. I never want to let go. We made love more times than I can count in the past couple of days. When we finally fell into bed exhausted around three this morning, I made sure she was locked tight in my arms. I don't know how long it's going to be before I get another chance like this with her. My plan still stands, though. I intend to fight for her. Fight for us.

The car pulls up outside the airport, and I'm grateful we're on a private flight. I get a little longer to pretend she's mine. Pretending, despite us both knowing the truth.

We're not really pretending.

With my hand on the small of her back, I guide her up the steps and onto the plane. "I'm gonna need you close, Cass," I say, my lips next to her ear.

She looks over her shoulder, eyebrows raised. "You're not sick of me yet?" She laughs. It's not her "I think I'm funny" laugh. No, this one is awkward, uncomfortable.

I know she's deflecting, and I'm not letting her. "Nope. I already told you that's not going to happen."

I don't miss the blush on her cheeks when she takes a seat, and I sit down next to her. We buckle up, and since we're on a private flight, we're in the air in no time at all. "Ready to be home?" she asks, wringing her hands together. She's nervous.

"Yes and no. I miss the kids." I chuckle fondly. "Never thought I'd be saying that, but those little buggers have wormed their way into my chest." I place my hand over my heart.

"They're adorable."

"On the other hand"—I reach over and wrap my fingers around her small hand—"there's the fact that I no longer get to do this whenever I want. I no longer get to kiss you or wake up wrapped around you."

"I'll miss this," she confesses.

"I'll miss you. The rest of it is just a bonus on top of getting to be with you. That's unless you've changed your mind?"

"No." She shakes her head. "No, I still think going back to... before is best."

My thumb rubs over her knuckles. No time like the present to let her know that I lied. "Yeah, I'm really not digging that plan anymore."

Her head whips around to face me. "W-what do you mean?"

Reaching over, I smooth her wild curls from her eyes. "What I mean is what I said. That plan, it's no longer appealing to me. Anything that keeps me from you is kind of on my shit list."

"Gavin." She closes her eyes, sucking in a deep breath and slowly exhaling. All I want to do is run my tongue over the column of her throat, feel her pulse under my tongue.

"Cassidy." I mimic her tone.

"We talked about this."

"We did, but I lied."

"What do you mean you lied? What are you talking about?"

"I lied to you. It's the first, and the last time I'll ever do it, but I knew if I told you how I felt you would have put a stop to our little getaway, and no way was I going to miss out on that time with you. So I lied."

She's staring at me, her eyes locked on mine as she tries to work this out in her head. "I—" She starts then stops. "We can't do this." She says the words, but there is no fight in her. She wants this as much as I do.

"We can do this. We've proved that we're amazing together. It's not just chemistry, Cass. It's more than that. Feelings are involved. The kind of feelings that cause my chest to tighten with just the mere thought of you or the sound of your name. The kind of feelings that make a man lie to a woman, just to get more time with her. I want you. I'm not going to stop wanting you. I'll do whatever it takes to make you see that. To see that everything will be okay. Your job, your mom, all of it will be okay. We're going to be okay."

"You don't know that," she says softly.

I cup her cheek. "I do know that, baby. I just need you to get on board with the plan. I won't stop until you're mine," I insist.

"You don't know how this will end. Ending it now, we're in control."

"That's where you're wrong," I say, leaning in and pressing a kiss to her forehead. "We're not in control here, not anymore. Our hearts are in control and I'm good with that. I'm good with following my heart. Are you?" I know she's going to say no. Her fear is keeping her from going all in. I get it. I understand why she worries. I get that it was just the two of them when she was growing up. I understand her hesitation, but that doesn't mean that I'm not going to do everything within my power to make her see things from my perspective.

"Gavin." She buries her face in her hands. "I want to, but I just can't. No, that's not true. I won't. I won't risk her care. She sacrificed for me, and that's what I'm going to do for her. I know it's hard for you to understand, but—" She stops when I place my finger over her lips.

"I'll show you." I drop my hand from her face, and lace my fingers through hers, gripping it tightly. "Now come here." I give her hand a gentle tug, pulling her into my lap. "I only have the rest of this flight to hold you like there's nobody watching. I plan to take full advantage of that."

"Gavin, we have to talk about this," she says, leaning her head against my chest.

"Nothing to talk about, Cass. I want you. You're scared, so it's my job to eliminate that fear. It's going to take some time, but I promise you. This, right here, right now, this will be us. I won't stop until you can see that. Until you know that we're in this together."

"I—"

I cut her off by pressing my mouth to hers. "No talking, more kissing. I need this flight to hold me over." I nip at her bottom lip, soothing it with my tongue. Her body relaxes as she opens for me. I spend the remainder of our flight touching her, kissing her sweet lips, and just holding her close. I have a fight on my hands, but this is Cassidy, my girl, nothing has ever been more worth it.

I've thought of a million different scenarios, all I need to run past my attorney. Like setting up a contract that I pay for her mother's care in the assisted-living facility for as long as she's there. One that secures her job with Soul Records until she decides otherwise.

"What are you thinking about?"

I turn to look at her, and even though I don't know how it all would work, I go with honesty. "We could write up a contract that says your job is secure, you know? Something that says no matter how this turns out, that you have a place at Soul Records."

"Gavin, I couldn't be there and not be with you."

I ignore that, because it's a nonissue. I know I'll never want anyone but her. "What if we had a contract that states I'm responsible for your mother's care in the event that you are unable to pay? That way you know that she's always going to be taken care of?" I hold my breath while I wait for her to process my words.

Tears well in her eyes. "You're an amazing man, Gavin McIntosh, but I can't let you do that. For a multitude of reasons."

I cradle her face in my hands. "I'd do it for you, for us. It's a small price to pay to be with you. Let's not forget to mention that it's not going to be needed. I'm never letting you go, Cass."

Her eyes close as she pulls out of my hold, resting her head against my shoulder. I don't push the issue any further. I need to talk to my attorney and see what we can work out. Placing my arm over her shoulders, I hold her close the rest of the flight.

When the plane lands, I kiss her one more time, just a peck to her lips, but it's enough—for now. We both know what it means. Back to Gavin and Cassidy before St. Louis. The us before I knew what it felt like to be inside of her. The us before I knew what it was like to sleep with her in my arms and wake up the same way. The only problem with that is I know now, and no way am I going to forget. Instead, I'm going to show her and everyone around us that she's my girl. No way in hell can I live without the taste of her lips against mine. I'll never force her, but I'm bringing my A game.

The drive to her place is silent. My hand is on her leg, because I can't not touch her, not when it's just the two of us. When the car stops outside of her place, my chest deflates. This is it. I have to let her go. I have to go back to wanting her but not being able to have her.

"So, I'll see you at the office tomorrow?" she asks.

I tug on one of her curls. "Yeah, that is unless you want to see me sooner?" It's less than twenty-four hours away, as our flight was early and I'm already dreading not being with her.

"I have a lot to do. Laundry, and I need to go visit Mom."

"I can go with you," I offer.

"No," she says quickly. "No, I should go alone. It's been a while since I've been there and she gets confused."

"I've been with you before."

"I'm sure you have better things to do."

"Than spend time with you? Not a chance."

"Gavin, we agreed," she reminds me.

"Nope. You agreed. I pretended to. I told you, I'm going to convince you that we're worth the risk, Cass. I intend to do just that."

"I'll see you tomorrow," she says, climbing out of the car. I follow behind her and help her with her bags.

"I'll take them up."

"No." She stops and turns to face me. "No, Gavin. I'm fine. Thank you for the offer, but we can't do this. We're home now and you need to go. Please." Her lip quivers. "Please just go."

"Cass…." I reach for her, but she steps to the side, preventing me from touching her. "Okay," I say reluctantly. "I'll see you tomorrow." My hands rest at my sides and I clench my fists to keep from reaching for her again. Everything in me is screaming to not let her out of my sight. To not let her forget our time together.

She nods, turns, and walks away. I watch her until I can no longer see her. This is going to be harder than I thought. I know I can't force it, but fuck me, it hurts like a bitch to watch her walk away.

CHAPTER 16

SPENT THE REST OF the day yesterday pretending that today was just another day at the office. A day where I would go in, do my job that I love, and pretend that when Gavin would flirt or casually brush up against me, that I didn't want him. Pretending. I've been doing a lot of that lately and today is going to be my biggest performance yet. I have to act as though I don't know what it's like to have his hands all over me. I have to forget what it felt like for him to have me pinned against the shower wall. There's a reason I never became an actress.

Fake it until you make it.

I'm terrible at faking it.

I spent the majority of the day visiting Mom. She didn't remember me either day, but she was having good days, so I'm happy with that. Seeing her get upset or agitated cracks my heart wide open. I hurt for her, for everything she's missing out on. She busted her ass to give me all she could and now that I've made it on my own, now that we have the financial freedom to enjoy the finer things in life, she can't.

I'm running late, which is something that I never do, but sleep has evaded me since the last night I could sleep without Gavin. If you'd have told me that I would have grown used to him and the warmth of him wrapped around me in just three nights, I'd have laughed at you. Now, I stand corrected. I did get used to it, used to him, and I miss him more than I ever thought possible. Even with that knowledge, I wouldn't have changed a thing about my time with him. Unless, it was that our trip was extended.

Hitting the opener on my visor, I drive into the underground parking lot that's housed under Soul Records. It's a perk of the job and I'm grateful to not have to find a place to park in downtown Nashville. Grabbing my bag, purse, keys, and phone, I head to the elevator that will take me up to my office. I'm cursing myself for not getting my ass in gear sooner. I'm missing my morning coffee.

When I step off the elevator, the office is quiet. I'm usually the first one in each day and most of the time the last to leave. The guys don't come in every day, well, except Gavin. Walking toward my office, I see the dim glow of my desk lamp. I slow my steps as I never leave it on. When I get closer, I hear a foot tapping and even without seeing him, I just know that it's Gavin. He's forever tapping out a beat that's running through his head. Taking a deep breath, I walk into my office, turning on the light as I go.

"Morning, beautiful," Gavin says softly.

"Gavin." I have yet to look at him but know that I need to. I also know that it's better I do it while it's just the two of us, but I can already feel my heart twisting. I don't want to just look at him. I want to wrap my arms around his waist and bury my face in his chest. I want that and so much more.

Schooling my features, I look up at him and smile. "Morning," I say, before looking back to my bag and busy myself removing and setting up my laptop.

"I brought you breakfast. And this." He reaches down to the floor and produces a drink carrier housing a tall coffee. I know without asking it's black just like I love it.

"How did you know?" I ask him.

He shrugs. "I know you, Cassidy. I know that you spent a lot of time over the weekend chastising yourself for the time we shared while we were away. I know that you spent as much time as you could with your mom, and I know that you didn't sleep well last night."

"H-how could you possibly know that?"

He frowns. "I know that, Cass, because I can't sleep a fucking wink without you. I reach for you and you're not there."

I nod. "Yeah, who would have thought?" I laugh humorlessly.

"Me, baby. I didn't have to think about it. I knew it was going to happen. For both of us," he adds.

Falling into my chair, I rest my elbows on my desk and bury my face in my hands. "How are we going to do this, Gavin? I have to sleep. I have to function without you."

He stands and kneels next to me. When he pulls my chair out, my hands drop into my lap. "It's selfish of me to say this, but you don't have to, Cass. I promise you, if you give in to this—" He runs his large calloused hands on my thighs. Thankfully, I'm wearing dress pants today. I don't know that I would be able to resist his hands on my bare skin. "You'll never have to be without me ever again."

I'm already shaking my head before he's finished talking. "You can't promise that, Gavin. Besides, we've been over this."

"We have and I told you, I'm fighting. I'm not giving up, not until you're tucked in close every damn night." He stands. Leaning down, he presses his lips to my temple. "Have a good day, baby."

"So damn insistent," I murmur as I watch him walk out the door. Grabbing the bag, I pull out my two glazed doughnuts, and a smile tilts the corner of my lips. He really does know me. Sometimes I wonder if he knows me better than I know myself.

After devouring my glazed doughnuts and half of my black coffee, I almost feel human. I get to work putting together a presentation from the bands I recorded at the festival. That's when I realize I only recorded two. "Shit," I mumble.

"What's up?" Logan's voice greets me from the doorway.

"Oh, you know, just having one of those days." Logan and I are close, but I don't think I can tell her, one of my boss's wives, that I hooked up with one of my other bosses and didn't do what they paid me to do. Yeah, not a good plan. I swear my life is starting to sound like bad reality television.

"Anything I can do to help?" she asks, stepping in further and taking the same seat where Gavin sat in earlier.

"No."

"Cassidy." She says my name just like my mother used to.

"You really have this Mom gig down tight." I laugh and so does she.

"I'm not trying to be your mom. I'm your friend. Tell me what's going on."

"I can't."

"Sure, you can. Besides, I'm sure I already know."

"Oh, you think so." I sit back in my chair and cross my arms over my chest. "Let's hear it."

"You sure?" she asks, smirking.

"Try me." I chuckle.

Standing from her chair, she surprises me when she shuts the door and turns the lock. "Better," she says, smiling.

"Now you're just starting to freak me out."

She throws her head back and laughs. "Nothing to worry about, I assure you. You ready?" She rubs her hands together as if telling me what she thinks is wrong with me is exciting to her. If she only knew.

"Yep."

"Here goes. You're in love with Gavin, he's in love with you. I can only guess that something happened while the two of you were away, which I was rooting for by the way. Now, you're living in a state of regret and if I'm to guess, fantasy."

"F-fantasy?" I ask, because really there is no use in denying it. I'm a shit liar.

"Yeah, you know, dreaming about your time with him, wanting to go back. Wanting one more touch, one more kiss, one more day." She shrugs.

I try to respond but end up looking like a fish out of water with my mouth opening and closing. Finally, I give up and just move my head from side to side. I'm at a loss as to how she knows all this.

"Relax, Cassidy. I'm observant, and well, the girls and I have been rooting for the two of you for a while now."

"W-what?" Did I hear her right?

"You heard me." She answers what I thought was a silent question. "Before you go freaking out, let me remind you that I was in your shoes not long ago."

"This is different. You didn't know that Kacen was your new boss," I point out.

"Semantics." She waves her hands through the air as if brushing me off. "What I want to know is why you're fighting it? Oh, and I assume from your shocked expression, I nailed it?" She grins.

"Pretty much." I fall back against my chair. "I tried to fight it while we were gone, I did, Logan, but he's Gavin and… yeah, I lost that battle."

"Go on," she says, still grinning.

"Where are the kids?"

"With Kace at the house. I told him I had some errands to run, which I do, but I really wanted to get you alone."

"Gavin's here," I remind her.

"Yeah, but we locked him out. Besides, if he happens to hear us, it's not a big deal. He knows what's going on. Although, I have a feeling the others suspect. The guys I mean. Lauren and Stacy are on my team. We've been planning and plotting. Who do you think put the idea in Kacen's head to send you all by yourselves?"

"You?"

She chuckles again. "You're welcome. So yeah, my husband might suspect, but he never tells me no." Her smile is blinding. "Now stop stalling, I need details."

"I fought it. The first night, I fought it, but damn it was hard. We had such a great day, just seeing the sites, and there's this graffiti wall and the arch. The second day we were there, we went to the festival early, and we were having another amazing day together. We were trying different beers, and he walked with me through all of the booths. Then we watched the bands, and the crowds were crazy, and he held me in front of him. One thing led to another, and we agreed to one night. Then one night turned into the rest of the time we were away. We didn't leave the hotel, and now I'm trying to compile the bands we saw and discovered I was so wrapped up in Gavin, so wrapped up in pretending, that I only recorded two of them."

"Was one of them Shattered Heart?" she asks.

"Yeah, I have a ton of footage of them, but just one other. The guys are going to be pissed."

"Cassidy, you were there to see Shattered Heart. That's why we sent you. You make a kickass presentation about the band, refer to their website, YouTube whatever you have to do, and they won't notice. You can speak about the other band, but really, they only want one."

"Are you sure about that?"

"I am, and if you were not beating yourself up so much, you would be, too."

"What am I going to do, Logan?"

"What do you want to do, Cassidy?" She answers my question with one of her own.

"Real talk?" I ask, and she nods. "I want to be with him. I want to be able to sleep at night because he's there beside me. However, I need this job, Logan. My mom needs me to keep this job."

"I think I'm proof that your job is safe."

"For now," I say. "What happens when this ends, whatever it is? Then what? I know that I can't be here and be around him and not be with him."

"What makes you think it's going to end?"

"I don't," I confess. It's the first time I've truly admitted to myself that there is another side of the what-if game. What if Gavin and I work out? What if we build a happy life together? I'm afraid to think about that side of the fence, knowing my heart can't take it. "But it's the risk… the chance that it could that stops me. She gave up so much for me, Logan," I say, fighting back the tears. I've played different scenarios a million different ways in my mind, and they all come back to Mom and the sacrifices she made for me.

"I understand, I do. You know what Kacen and I went through. But let me ask you this. What about this scenario? The one where you and Gavin build a life together? Think about that, about the outcome of that."

"That's a dream come true," I respond immediately, not even having to think about it. "I've thought about it, but it's still a risk. I can't sacrifice her care. I just can't."

"Yeah, and dreams do come true, Cassidy. You have to stop fighting the unknown. You have to open yourself up to the possibilities, *all* possibilities. Not just the 'what happens when this ends' but the 'what happens when we live happily ever after?'"

"You know what I wish? I wish my mom knew who I was. I wish I could talk to her about Gavin. I wish she could tell me what she would do."

"I'm sorry, sweetie. I know you miss her, and I can't imagine her being here in body but not in mind. My heart breaks for both of you. As a mother myself, I'm pretty sure I can tell you what she would say."

"Yeah? What's that?" I ask, even though deep down I already know as well.

"She would tell you to follow your heart. Love is a gift, one that is rare and precious. She would tell you to take the chance, to fall head first and hope that he catches you and if he doesn't, even though we both know he will, you are a strong, beautiful woman and you will be okay."

My eyes fill with tears. "Like I said, you got this mom thing nailed down tight." I choke out a watery laugh.

"Think about it. I'm here if you need to talk. We need a girls' night soon. I'll call Stacy and Lauren and set something up." I stand and hug her goodbye before she unlocks the door and lets herself out. "Hey, Gav," she says, and I know we're busted.

CHAPTER 17

GAVIN

H AVING GIVEN CASS TIME TO eat and consume some coffee, I head back to her office to see if she needs any help with the presentation on Shattered Heart. Her office door's shut. Hearing voices, I listen closer and immediately recognize Logan. Instead of walking away like I should, I lean against the wall and listen to their conversation. I'm not ashamed to admit that I do a little jig here in the hallway when I hear Logan, the other girls, and even the guys are rooting for us. Not that I thought they wouldn't be. We're family.

I hear the emotion in Cass's voice and want to break down the door to get to her, to hold her and tell her that it will all be okay. That if she just lets me, I'll love her until the end of time, and that the what-ifs are nonexistent. All she needs to worry about is where she wants to live and how many babies we're going to have. My vote is lots, or as many as she's willing to give me.

Their conversation comes to an end, and I rush to the opposite side of the wall.

Leaning my back against it, I cross my arms and legs. I'm going for casual, but I know they'll both be able to see right through me.

"Hey, Gav." Logan winks and smiles as she heads down the hall.

"Give that baby a hug from Uncle Gav," I yell after her.

"Come by and see him he misses you," she replies over her shoulder, before disappearing on the elevator.

Looking up, I see Cass watching me, biting her bottom lip. "Easy, baby," I say, walking toward her. Gently, I press on her bottom lip with my thumb, and she releases it. "What's wrong?"

"I only recorded two bands."

I nod. "That's fine. We really only wanted to see Shattered Heart anyway. Can I help?"

"No. Yes. Hell, I don't know." She closes her eyes and takes a deep breath.

"Hey." I wrap my arm around her waist and pull her into my chest. I expect her to remind me that we shouldn't or pull away. Instead, she surprises me when she buries her face in my chest.

"This is harder than I thought it would be, Gavin. I can still feel your lips on mine. I can feel your hands on every inch of my skin. I miss your warmth and this, you holding me… I didn't know it would be this hard."

"We can fix that, Cass. You and me. Say the word, and I'll fix it for you. I just need you to tell me."

Her cell phone rings, causing her to pull away and retreat to her office. I follow her; we're not done here.

"This is Cassidy," she greets.

I watch her closely, taking the opportunity to allow my eyes to roam over her body. When her face pales and her legs wobble so much that she has to hold on to her desk to keep from falling, I rush to her side and wrap her in my arms. Tears, big crocodile tears roll down her cheeks, so I take the phone from her.

"Hi, this is Gavin McIntosh. Can you tell me what's going on?" I ask the person on the other end of the line.

"Mr. McIntosh. This is Marcy from the Better Living Assisted Living. I was calling to talk to Cassidy about her mother."

"She's upset. You can tell me whatever you need to. I'll be sure to relay the message or do whatever it is we need to do."

"I'm sorry, sir, family only," she says, and I can hear the regret in her voice.

"Cass is my fiancée," I say without thinking. It's not a farfetch from how I see her in my mind anyway.

"Oh," she says, surprise in her voice. "Well, Mrs. Hillman has been taken to the hospital. She had an accident. We found her in her room. She's taken a fall. It appears that she may have had a stroke."

A sob escapes from Cassidy's lips, and I hold her a little tighter. "Which hospital?" I ask. I listen as she tells me which hospital and that the ambulance left no more than five minutes ago. "We're on our way." I end the call, sliding her phone in my pocket before wrapping both arms around her. "I got you, Cass. I know you're worried and upset, but we need to go to her, okay?" My voice is soft and calm.

"Is she—" She swallows back another sob. "—is she gone?"

"No, baby. Come on, we need to go. I'll explain on the way." I grab her purse from her desk and guide her to the elevator. In the parking garage, I help her into my truck before rushing to the driver's side. "They found her on the floor of her room. They think she had a stroke," I explain. She nods, letting me know she heard me. Reaching over, I lace her fingers through mine, cursing the fact that I don't have a bench seat in the front of my truck.

Touching the phone icon on my steering wheel, I instruct my hands-free system to call Kacen. It only rings once before he's picking up. "What's up, G?" he asks.

"Hey, I'm on my way to the hospital with Cassidy. She just got a call that her mom took a fall. I left the label, we hadn't unlocked any doors, but I don't know what's on the schedule for today. Can you—"

"I'm all over it, my man. What else do you need?"

"Can I get back to you on that?"

"Yeah. Keep me posted."

"Will do." I hit the phone icon again to end the call. The drive to the hospital takes about twenty minutes due to morning traffic. The entire drive, Cass grips my hand as her silent tears coat her cheeks. I hate this for her and wish I could take the pain. I pray her mom is okay and can bounce back from this.

Pulling into the lot, Cassidy jumps out of the truck, and I scramble to grab her purse, my phone, and keys to follow after her. To my surprise, she's standing outside the Emergency Room doors just staring at them. "Come on," I urge her with my hand on the small of her back. Her feet don't move. I stand in front of her and cup her face in my hands. "I'm not leaving you, baby. We need to go in and see what's going on. You with me?"

"I'm scared," she whispers.

"I'm right here and am not leaving you."

A subtle nod is all I get as she takes one step and then another until we're through the doors and standing in front of the receptionist. "Hi, Margaret Hillman, this is her daughter. We got a call that they brought her here."

"Name?" the lady behind the desk asks.

"Cassidy Hillman," I tell her.

"Down the hall and to the left is a private waiting room. You can wait there. I'll let the doctor know you're here."

"Oh, God," Cass sobs, her hands covering her mouth.

My hand, which is resting on the small of her back, wraps around her waist and pulls her close. "Breathe, baby. We don't know anything yet. I'm sure they never talk to families in the waiting room. There are laws against that."

"She was fine yesterday. I mean, she didn't know me, but that's nothing new. She was in good spirits."

"Come here." I take a seat in the waiting room and pull her down onto my lap. I don't say anything, and neither does she. I hold her close, running my hands up and down her back to soothe her. And we wait.

"Family of Margaret Hillman," a doctor in a long white coat asks as he enters the room. He's older, graying hair at his temples. I watch him, trying to read his facial expression. He doesn't look as though he's about to deliver us a blow of bad news.

"Me," Cass says, standing on shaking legs. I stand with her, placing my arm around her waist, silently letting her know I'm here. "I'm her daughter."

"And you?" he says to me.

"I'm her fiancé." I stick to my story. Cass doesn't even blink an eye as she stares at the doctor, waiting for any scraps of information he can give us.

"Right, it appears Mrs. Hillman has suffered a stroke. We're still running some tests to see what damage, if any, has occurred."

"She's okay?" Cassidy's small voice asks.

"Yes. She's going to be fine. Although, there might be damage from the stroke. In some cases paralysis and memory loss."

"She has Alzheimer's," she tells him.

"Yes. And although that is the case, on her good days, she might not remember as much as she did before."

"The good days are few and far between," she says, wiping her tears. "When can I see her?"

"We have a few more tests to run, then we will put her in a room. I want to keep her overnight for observation, just to be safe."

"Do we know what caused this? Is there anything that we can do to prevent it from happening again?" I ask him. Whatever it is, I plan to make it happen.

His eyes soften. "Unfortunately, there's nothing for prevention. We will start her on medication, but that's not 100 percent effective."

"Thank you, Doctor." I hold my hand out and he accepts it. "We'll be here when she's in her room." With a nod, he's out the door as quickly as he arrived.

I guide Cass to the row of chairs and set her down on my lap once again. I need to hold her and give her all my strength right now. Her face is buried in my chest, and her grip on my shirt is tight. I close my eyes and rub my hand up and down her back. It's not until I hear a throat clear that my eyes snap open and I see the guys and Logan standing in the doorway watching us. Cass moves to get up and I lock my arms around her. "Stay, baby."

"Hey." Logan takes the seat next to us. "How are you holding up?" she asks Cassidy.

"I'm doing okay. It was a stroke." She goes on to tell her everything the doctor just told us. "Where are the kids?" she asks.

"Stacy and Lauren are watching Drew at Cole and Stacy's with Zach and Riley."

Kacen takes the seat next to his wife and wraps his arm around her shoulders. "Drew was in big brother mode when we left." He chuckles. "He loves to feed the babies. I'm telling you, he needs a sibling," Kacen tells his wife, causing us all to laugh.

"I've been telling Lauren the same thing," Tristan adds.

"Trust me, as soon as I can get Stacy on board, it's happening." Cole grins.

"Hey now," Logan speaks up. "Give the girl a break. He's three weeks old," she counters.

"I know and can't wait to do it all over again."

"You guys." Cassidy sits up on my lap, but my arms are around her waist, so she can't move. I want her right where she's at. "You didn't have to come down here. I'm good, promise."

"Bullshit," Cole says. "Cassidy, you're family. Not just part of the Soul Records family, but by the looks of the way my boy has you on lockdown, you're in deeper than that. We take care of our family." She drops her head to look at her lap and her shoulders begin to shake. "Shit, I'm sorry, Cassidy, I didn't mean to upset you."

She shakes her head. "No, it's not that. She's—" She stops to gather herself. "She's the only family I have left. It's just been the two of us as long as I can remember."

I pull her close, placing my lips to her ear. "Not anymore," I say, at the exact same time Kacen, Logan, Tristan, and Cole say the exact same thing.

A sob breaks from her chest, and I pull her close. She latches onto my shirt and lets her tears fall.

"We're going to go grab some coffees. We'll be back," Logan says softly. I nod and watch as she points to the door and my three best friends, my brothers, follow her out.

I knew they would react that way, that they would accept her into our family with no questions asked. I'm glad she got to see it as well. I just wish it were under better circumstances.

CHAPTER 18

 *Cassidy*

AVIN'S HOLD ON ME NEVER wavers as I grip his shirt and let my emotions get the best of me. For so long it's been the two of us, my mom and me. I've handled these trips on my own before today. Calls in the middle of the night, falls, spells, illness… all of it, I was alone. Then today, he was there, and with him comes this amazing group of people. I know them more than just as my employers and their families. I *know* them. I know that Logan wants another baby just as badly as Kacen does. I know that Stacy, although she might pretend otherwise, would be thrilled to have another baby just like little Riley. I know that Lauren and Tristan are trying for number two now. I know all that because I've become friends with them. Somehow, I missed it. Between the phone calls, the chats in the office, the invites to barbecues, birthday parties, and baby showers, I somehow missed the bigger picture. These people are not my work colleagues, they're *my* family.

What makes it worse is that Gavin has been trying to tell me that all along. That no matter how things might or might not turn out with us, that won't change. I'm an idiot. I've been so wrapped up in Mom's sacrifices for me, I failed to notice that I do have more than her. They might not be blood relatives, but I know without a shadow of a doubt if I need them, they'd be here for me.

INSISTENT

Lifting my head, I look at Gavin. His eyes are trained on me. "You okay, baby?" he asks, pushing my hair out of my eyes.

"Yeah." I sit up and place my hands on his cheeks. "I'm so sorry, Gavin. I've been pushing you away. No matter how bad I wanted to pull you close, I had myself convinced I couldn't have you. I was convinced I would lose them when I lost you."

"That's ridiculous. They love you."

"Of course, we do," Tristan says from the doorway. He walks toward us and sets two coffees down on the small table before taking the seat next to us. "I've watched him for months now." He points to Gavin. "He's the first to volunteer with anything that has to do with the studio, and although he's technically single, he never once complains about us staying in with our wives and kids. I should have seen it sooner. It wasn't that he was just being nice, since we now have our own families, although that is part of it. It was you. He wanted to spend more time with you. We all knew there was someone. We just didn't know who. Not until the girls started dropping hints." He grins. "G, he was there for me when Zach was born. They all were, but G stepped up, and until now, I didn't know how I would ever repay him. Let me tell you what I'm sure my brother has already said, but the way I see it. Cassidy, he loves you. We all see it. Trust me on this one. Don't fight it. Life is a precious gift, and you never know when that will be challenged." His eyes go dark, and I know he's thinking about how he almost lost his wife and son. "If my wife is right, and she's always right, you love him, too." He stands and walks away. "We're going to grab something to eat. We'll bring you something back." And with that, he's out the door and leaving us alone.

Gavin is quiet, and so am I. I think about how it feels to be with him, to know that I can lean on him and that he'll always be there. I want that forever. I want to be able to know I have his strength, and in turn give him mine.

"I'm sorry, Gavin," I whisper.

"Baby, you have nothing to be sorry for. Let's just worry about getting your mom better."

"No." I sit up and slide off his lap, taking the seat next to us that Tristan just left. I need a clear head for this, and that can't happen with him touching me. "I'm sorry for pushing you away. I was wrong, so very wrong." I pause, and when he reaches for my hand, I let him lace his

96

fingers through mine. "I don't know why I couldn't or didn't see it before now, but I've been so wrong. My focus has been on my mom, on what she gave up for me. I was too honed in on the fact that I'm all she has, to realize that when she's gone, I'm alone. I have no one. That phone call today, although it was like many others I've received in the past couple of years, it did more than scare me that I'd lost her this time. It opened my eyes. Maybe it was my talk with Logan earlier, maybe it was the time we spent together last week…? Probably a combination of everything but what I realize is that I need you."

"Cass," he whispers and reaches for me, but I lean back.

"I'm sorry for putting us through that, for pushing when all I wanted to do was pull. I wanted to pull you into me and hold on tight."

"I'm right here," he says softly.

"Do you still want me, Gavin? Can you forgive me for all the heartache I've put us through?"

"There's nothing to forgive." He reaches for me again, and this time, I let him. He has me back in his lap, his arms locked around my waist, and his face buried in my neck. "There's something I need," he murmurs.

"What's that?" I ask, running my fingers through his hair.

"I need you to say it."

"Can you look at me?" I ask. I need to see his eyes when I do it. He lifts his head, and his blue eyes are darker than I've ever seen them. "I want to be yours."

"You've always been mine." He leans in and presses a kiss to my lips. When he pulls back, he studies me. "This is open, right? We don't have to hide, and I don't have to pretend like I'm not madly in love with you?"

My breath hitches in my chest. "W-what did you just say?" I know what he said, but I need to hear it one more time. Just for clarification.

"Cassidy Hillman, I'm madly and irrevocably in love with you." His smile is bright and my heart is full.

"I love you, too."

"Excuse me," a female voice says from the doorway. "Ms. Hillman, we have your mother moved to a room. Would you like to see her?"

"Yes." I stand. "Is she awake?"

She smiles. "She is. She's been asking for you."

I can't help but perk up at that. She's asking for me? That means she remembers me. Those days are rare as of late. "Thank you." I step toward her. Gavin grabs my hand and moves up beside me. Hand-in-hand we follow the nurse out of the waiting room. Logan, Kacen, Cole, and Tristan are walking up the hall. "She's awake." I smile through my tears. I don't stop walking and neither does Gavin as we head toward her room.

"That's great news," Logan says. They turn and follow us down the hall and onto the elevator.

"I'm sorry, but when we get to Mrs. Hillman's room, it's two at a time, and immediate family only," the nurse says.

"We are her family," Tristan pipes up. "There're a lot more of us too, so you might want to warn the other nurses."

Gavin chuckles, throwing his arm over my shoulder as we follow the nurse out of the elevator. When we get to her room, he removes his arm, and kisses my temple. "I'll be right outside."

"No." I grab onto his arm. "I want you to go in with me."

His eyes soften and he nods. "Okay."

As simple as that. I need him and he's there. I push open the door and see Mom's frail frame lying in the hospital bed. Tears well in my eyes, but I push them away. I need to be strong for her. Gavin gives my hand a squeeze, and I pull from his strength. "Hey, Mom," I whisper. I don't know what state of mind she's in and the last thing that I want to do is scare her or get her agitated. All I know is that she was asking for me, and I pray that I get to have her lucid, for just a little while.

"Cassidy, my baby." She holds her hand out for me, and I drop Gavin's and rush to her side, losing the battle with my tears. "I'm sorry I scared you," she says when I take her hand in mine.

I shake my head and smile. "How are you feeling?" There are a million things I want to ask her. A million and one things that I want to tell her. I don't know how long her lucid state will be here for and I miss her. I miss my mother.

"I'm fine. Don't fuss," she says, looking over my shoulder. "You again?" she asks.

Gavin clears his throat and steps up behind me. "Hello, Margaret," he says.

"I've seen you before."

"Yes, ma'am. I'm Cassidy's boyfriend, Gavin." His voice is strong and full of conviction. She's the first person we got to tell, and my heart is full because of it.

"You did good, sweetheart." Mom smiles.

An abrupt laugh spills out of my mouth. "Yeah." I look to the side and smile at Gavin. "Yeah, I did."

"You two will make beautiful babies," Mom adds, and I feel the blush coat my cheeks.

"Mom," I scold her.

"She's right, Cass, we would," Gavin says with a wink.

"I'm not getting any younger you know." There's an amused glint in her eyes that I haven't seen in so long. It's so beautiful I capture it to my memory.

"Right again, Cassidy. You know, you should really listen to your mother," he says, his face stone serious.

Before I can reply, a nurse steps in. "I'm sorry to interrupt, Ms. Hillman, I have a few papers for you to sign."

I look at Mom and back to Gavin. "Go on." She waves me off. "Gavin and I will get to know one another."

I turn to look at him. "We'll be right here when you come back." He leans in and kisses my cheek, then steps back so I can follow the nurse out into the hallway.

CHAPTER 19

GAVIN

I DON'T TAKE MY EYES off her until she's out the door. Part of me wants to chase after her and glue myself to her side. I just got her, officially, and I don't need her changing her mind. Not that I think she would. I can feel in her touch she's felt this way for a while now but has fought it. She's not fighting anymore.

"You love her," Margaret says. Her voice is soft, weak.

"I do." She's lucid, and although I don't know where she goes when her mind wanders, I hope she knows that her daughter is loved and will always be taken care of.

"She loves you, too. I see it."

"She does. I'm a lucky man," I confess.

"What are your intentions with my daughter?" she asks, a small smile tilting her lips.

Here goes nothing. "I plan to marry her and give you those grandbabies you were just asking for." I put it out there, and it feels damn good to know we're finally both on the same path toward our future. "With your permission of course," I add. I don't need it, but I know that it would mean a lot to Cassidy.

She chuckles. "Promise me to love her with everything in you, and you have it."

"Wait." A thought hits me. I dig my cell phone out of my pocket. "Do you mind if I record this? I want to ask you again and have you tell me that or whatever version of that that you can. I want her to see this one day. I want her to know that you know she's being loved and taken care of. That she has my family and me, my friends to support her."

"That's a good idea," she says softly. "I don't know how much longer I'll be me, and I want that peace for her for when I'm not here."

I can't imagine what that must feel like. To know one day you're not going to know your loved ones the next. To not know how long you will remember your loved ones and the memories you've made. I can't fathom the worry and the pain knowing that when they come to see you, that you don't know who they are and you push them away.

"You're always you." I give her hand a gentle squeeze. "Ready?" I ask. She nods, and I hit Record on the camera, facing it toward her. "Margaret, I would like to ask your permission to marry your daughter. I love her. I want to give you and her those babies you were just talking about." I try to remember how our first conversation went, but this time I'm nervous. I don't know if it's because I started this conversation or the fact that one day, Cass will hear it. Or maybe it's because I want to marry her and have babies with her... yesterday in fact.

"You'll love her with everything you have? Love your babies just as fiercely?"

"You have my word."

"Yes." She looks at me for several long minutes and just as I'm about to end the recording, she starts speaking again. "I don't know if I'll remember this. I don't know if I will ever be me again after this. This disease, it's a terrible one, but there are a few things I want to say." She turns her face to look directly at the camera. "Cassidy, I love you, my sweet girl. You have given me so much joy in my life. I know we had some hard times when you were younger, but we always had each other. I want you to know that if I'm not here either in body or mind on your wedding day, that I'm there with you in spirit. I'm watching over you, and I'm so happy that you've found a man who loves you like Gavin does." She swallows hard.

"And the day you have your babies. I'll be there. I want so badly to see you as you go through the changes that pregnancy brings, to watch you be a mother, but I know the chances of that are slim. Instead, I'll be with you, watching you love those babies and that husband of yours. I want that for you, Cassidy. I want you to be happy and live a full life. I want you to not fret over the things I can't be there for, but for the memories you have. Keep them close to your heart and maybe share a few of our traditions with your own family. You know, making cookies over the holidays, making your Halloween costumes, camping out in the living room. When you do those things with your children, think of me. I'll be there with you, I promise you." She stops as her tears take over. I go to set my phone down, and she shakes her head. I keep it up, recording her tears as I feel my eyes well up with my own. "I love you, Cassidy. Be happy, my sweet girl. Love this man, and live each moment. I'll be there in your heart, in spirit. I'll always be there. I love you," she says, her voice cracking. This time I do end the recording. I shove my phone back in my pocket and grab her frail hands in mine.

"Thank you, Margaret. I promise you I will love her until the day I take my last breath." She smiles up at me and nods.

"Hey, everything okay?" Cass asks us. I pull away and blink back the emotions, not wanting her to see.

She steps up next to me, but I don't look at her, not yet. "Everything is fine. I was just telling your mom how fantastic her daughter is," I say, pulling her into my side and kissing her temple.

"Mom?" she inquires.

"Just a twinge of pain, sweet girl. I'll be fine," she assures her daughter.

"Uh-huh," she says, not really believing either of us, but letting it go. "So, they say you have to stay overnight. Then you can go back tomorrow."

"I'm fine here, you should go," her mom says.

"Not going to happen. Gavin, you can go back. I plan to stay here with Mom."

"I'll go tell the others, and then I'll be back. I'm staying with you."

"They're not going to let both of us stay."

"You let me worry about that." I flash her a grin and see the smile that she's fighting. In the waiting room, I find the guys and Logan. "Hey, she's good. Actually, really good right now. She's herself, which is an uncommon and a pleasant surprise all things considered. Cass needs that."

"How is Cassidy?" Logan asks.

"She's okay. Relieved. Spending some much-needed time with her mom while she can." I don't explain my statement. They all get it. "They're keeping her overnight just for observation. Y'all should go on home."

"Do you need anything?" Tristan asks.

"Nah. I'll run out and grab us some food and clothes. I'm staying with her."

"How does she feel about that?" Logan asks. I hear the concern in her voice.

I smile. I can't help it. "My girlfriend is fine with me staying. How else would she feel?" I throw it out there and it feels damn good, too.

"Does she know about that title?" Kacen laughs.

"Yep. So, does her mom. I'm stoked that she's lucid right now, so we at least had the chance to tell her. Thank you for being here."

"Call us if you need anything. Give them both a hug from us," Logan, ever the caretaker, says.

"Will do. I need to get back in there. Thanks again." I give the guys a handshake and hug Logan tightly before heading back to my girl. When I enter the room, Cass has the chair pulled up to the bed and they are talking softly. "Hey."

"Hey." Her smile is huge, and I know having her mom right now is the reason why. "I'm going to let the two of you catch up and run and get us some food. Do you need anything else?"

"Yeah, can you run by my place and get me something to change into? Something more comfortable than this?" I look down at her dress pants, silk shirt, and high heels. She's sexy as fuck.

"Yeah." I take the offered keys from her hands. "I'll be back soon. Margaret, can I bring you anything?"

"No, thank you." She yawns.

"Be back soon. Call me if you need me." I head to my place first, change quickly into some sweats and a hoodie, just in case. My next stop is Cass's place. I grab some of those tight pants her and the girls are always wearing, a T-shirt, some socks, shoes, and a hoodie, too. I swing through the drive-through and grab some burgers and fries, and I'm headed back to the hospital.

Cassidy is in the waiting room when I get there, tears rushing down her face. I hurry to her, dropping the food and the bag I packed for her onto the chair and wrap my arms around her. She holds on to me as if she never wants to let go. "What's wrong, Cass?"

"We were talking and then all of a sudden, she got confused. She didn't know who I was. She was angry that there was a stranger in her room. I tried to tell her it was me, but that only made it worse. She worked herself up so much they had to sedate her."

I hold her in my arms and wish I knew what to say. I wish I had words to comfort her. She doesn't need to hear that everything is going to be okay, I get that. I just don't know what I can say to help her through this. I hate it for both of them. This disease is gut-wrenching. When her tears slow, I pull back and wipe her cheeks. "Why don't you go get changed and we can eat?" I suggest.

She nods and grabs the bag from the floor, walking toward the small bathroom off the waiting room. When she gets to the door, she turns to face me. I know because I've not taken my eyes off her. "I love you, Gavin McIntosh." I don't get to tell her that I love her, too, before she disappears behind the door.

CHAPTER 20

THE LAST TWENTY-FOUR HOURS have been a roller coaster of emotions. Last night, Gavin and I stayed at the hospital. Mom slept most of the time and the moments she was awake, she didn't know who we were. I will forever cherish that small window of time where she was more than just the body of my mother, but the mind, too. I'm glad I got to introduce her to Gavin as my boyfriend and talk to her about how much he makes me feel. I told her about the shoes, the black patent leather ones that sit in the bottom of my closet. She laughed and told me to throw them away. That those shoes were a blip on the radar of the memories and sacrifices we made together. My mother is the greatest woman I've ever known. It tears me up inside not knowing if I will ever get a chance like that again. To sit and talk to her and her remember. I can only hope.

Throughout it all, Gavin has been by my side. Last night we slept in the waiting room. The lights were dim and he insisted on holding me in his arms. He had to be uncomfortable, but he was adamant there'd be no more nights where I wouldn't be sleeping in his arms. It was where I belonged. I didn't fight him. Truth be told, I needed him. I needed to feel his strength around me.

"You need anything from your place?" Gavin asks.

INSISTENT

We just left the assisted-living home where mom lives. She was released from the hospital earlier this afternoon. "Am I not going home?" I ask him.

"We both need sleep. We've already determined that neither of us can sleep without the other. We can go to your place if you prefer. We just have to swing by mine to get some clothes."

"I need clothes."

"Okay. We'll swing by your place first."

I don't argue with him. The weekend was long and sleepless thinking about him, wishing he'd been with me. He said the same. With last night us sleeping in a chair in the hospital waiting room, we're both dead on our feet.

When we pull up to my condo, we both climb out of the truck and head inside. I start down the hall to my bedroom, grabbing a bag out of the closet and start adding clothes to change into and something for work tomorrow.

"Go ahead and pack some extra," Gavin says.

Stopping what I'm doing, I look up at him. "Why?"

"So you can have a few things at my place. We'll be better prepared next time."

I open my mouth to argue with him and remember that I don't have to. Instead, I smile at him, turn back around, and add a few more items in my bag. After that, I head to my bathroom to get my toiletries. When I come back out, he's still standing there, arms and legs crossed, leaning against the doorjamb.

"Ready?" I ask, stopping to stand next to him. His answer is to slip his hand around my neck and bring me into a kiss. When he pulls back, I want to beg him to keep going, but I'm exhausted, and so is he.

On the drive to his place, I let the events of the last week run through my mind. Last week with Gavin was one I will never forget, and one I thought I would never have again. Then yesterday when I got the call, he was the one who I wanted with me, not only that, but he was there. It's funny how tragedy can make you see the forest through the trees.

Once we arrive at his place, he carries my bag into his room. I follow along behind him. I've been here before, but not in his room. *Never* in his room. When he disappears behind another door, I assume is the bathroom, I stand here, not really sure what to do with myself. Do I crawl into bed? Go back to the living room? I don't have to wonder long because he appears, naked as the day he was born with his hand held out for me.

"Shower, then bed. That hospital shower was shit."

I take his offered hand and let him guide me into the huge bathroom. It's bigger than I thought it would be for a condo. Then again, this is not your average condo. Gavin steps under the spray and I realize that I'm still standing here gawking at him and his bathroom. I quickly discard my clothes, leaving them in a pile on the floor next to his and step into the shower. I don't really know what I was expecting, but it wasn't to stand across from Gavin, both of us with our own shower heads, washing away the grime of the past twenty-four hours. Our eyes stay locked on one another, and if I weren't exhausted, it would be one hell of a foreplay session. I can see the heat in his eyes, but the exhaustion as well.

When we're finished, Gavin steps out first and wraps a towel around his waist. He then holds one open for me, and I step into it, into him. Once he has it secured around my waist, he gives me another for my hair. Something he learned during our week together. Then again, maybe it was another woman he learned that from.

"What were you thinking just now?" he asks.

"Nothing." I wave away his concern, leaning my head over and wrapping my hair up in the extra towel.

"Don't do that, Cass. Talk to me."

"Fine," I huff. "I was just thinking about how thoughtful it was that you got me another towel for my hair and that you must have learned that about me last week. Then I realized it might have been another woman who you've spent so much time with who taught you that we need two towels. I'm tired, and I was being stupid, I know." I wave my hands in the air. "It's nothing. Just ignore me."

"I'm not going to ignore you. That's not how this is going to work, Cass. You have something to say, you say it. If you're thinking something, no matter what it might be, you tell me. We work through it together. That's how this works. We're in this together," he says, stepping closer. "Let's get you dried off and in bed. Then we can talk."

The towel that's around my body falls open when he pulls at the piece that I had tucked in holding it up. Slowly, he runs the soft cotton over my skin, soaking up the remnants of our shower. "I'll get you something to sleep in while you do your hair," he says, tossing the towel in the basket and walking out of the room.

Dropping the towel from my hair, I'm too tired to do anything but brush it out, and I put in up in a knot on top of my head. It's sure to be a hot mess with a mass of frizzy curls when I wake up in the morning, but I couldn't care less. Sleep. What I need is sleep.

Turning off the light, I walk into the bedroom, and Gavin hands me a T-shirt. "Here."

"I brought sleep clothes." I point to my bag that sits on the chair in the corner of the room.

"Yeah, but this is better." He holds out his hand, offering me the shirt again.

I take it and slide it over my head. It's too big, reaching past mid-thigh, but it smells like him. It's an old Soul Serenade T-shirt, one from the early years. Turning off the lights, Gavin guides me with his hand on the small of my back to the bed. He pulls back the covers, and from the dim glow of the moonlight coming through the windows, I can see he's waiting for me to get in. I slide in, and the softness of the mattress surrounds me.

Gavin follows in after me, sliding the cover up over us. "Finally," he murmurs, pulling me into his arms and pressing a kiss to my temple. "Now, let's talk. First of all, there have been other women in my life. None of them important enough to remember. Second, I couldn't have given a fuck less what they liked and what they didn't. They served a purpose. Yes, I'm aware that makes me sound like a dick, but let's call a spade a spade. Third, you're the first woman I've brought there. This is my place, my home. I never brought randoms here, not ever. This is personal, and they were just sex." I try to speak, but he talks over me, so I wait. "Finally, it was all you. I wasn't sure when I would get this time with you again, so I soaked up as much of you as I could get. Remember things that you liked and disliked, trying to form a plan to lure you here. In my bed. For the rest of your life."

The rest of my life? I ignore that for now and go back to my original statement that he wouldn't let me make. "Sex is personal."

"Sex is intimate. Making love is personal. Even when I'm fucking you, I'm making love to you. There's a difference."

"Sex is sex, Gavin."

"That's where you're wrong. I never craved to have their pussies wrapped around my cock. I never wanted to taste them more than I needed my next meal. I never wanted to get lost in them," he says softly. "When I'm inside you, I feel like I lose a part of myself to you. And that's okay," he adds quickly. "I'm good with losing myself to you. I want that more than anything. That's personal, Cass. That's more than sex. That's love, baby."

He's right. My insecurities are showing. Instead of fighting with him, which is the last thing I want to do, I snuggle into his chest, place a kiss there, and whisper, "I love you." His breathing is smooth and even, his chest barely moving as I lie against him.

"This," he says, holding me a little tighter, "this is how you're supposed to fall asleep at night." His lips press to the top of my head. "I love you too, Cass."

That's the last thing I remember before drifting off into what turns out to be a peaceful night's sleep.

CHAPTER 21

GAVIN

I t's been a week today since Cass got the phone call that her mom was being rushed to the hospital. With the help of Logan, I was able to convince her to take the rest of the week off. We stayed at my place and went to see her mom every day. Not once in any of those days did she remember her, remember us. Cassidy acted as though she was okay with it, but I know better. I'm sure on some level, she's used to it, but that does not mean that she's okay with it. I wish there was something that I could do, something that could make her better.

I called around, spoke to a few specialists, and there's not much else they can do. There are some medication trials, but for the most part, this is the disease. Alzheimer's, in a way, is worse on the family than it is the patient. They don't know what they can't remember.

Today is the first day back at the label for both of us. Cassidy insisted on putting together the presentation on Shattered Heart to send to the other guys. I conceded because she did it sitting on my couch in nothing but one of my T-shirts and a pair of panties. If I had it my way, she'd work from my couch every day.

Today is the first day we're back to work as a couple. The guys and their wives all stopped by last week. Even Stacy and baby Riley came over to visit. They embraced our new relationship just as I thought they would—with open arms. Cass was nervous at first, but she soon realized there was nothing to be nervous about. She calmed down, and we enjoyed our week. That was until this morning. She's changed her outfit at least three times and changed her hair twice.

"I should have stayed at my place last night," she says, turning sideways to look at herself in the mirror. "I don't know if this is the right one." She sighs and lets her arms drop to her sides.

"Babe, do you normally have this much trouble getting ready for work?" I ask cautiously.

"No," she huffs. "This is not just another day, Gavin. This is us, going to the office as an *us*."

I remain where I am, sitting on the bed, staring at her through the open bathroom door. "Babe," I say carefully, not wanting to upset her further. This is new territory for me, but I've seen the guys with their wives, and I know Cass. "It's just us. Me, the guys, the girls, the kids. That's it. Nothing to be nervous about."

"I can't help it," she sighs. "It's what I've worried about forever, wanting you, but not being able to have you because of my job. I don't know how to let that go," she admits.

I stand and go to her, wrapping my arms around her waist. "Look," I say, pointing to the mirror in front of us. "That's us, babe. We're the same people as we were before, only better versions. At least, I'm a better version. We're good together. You kick ass at what you do and keeping the label running. That's all you have to do. Go to work, kick ass, and come home to me."

"Gavin, it's been a week since I've stayed at my place."

"Yeah, about that. You should just give up your condo," I tell her.

"What?" She turns in my arms and looks up at me.

"We both agree sleeping alone is not something either of us want to do, so why not?"

"Why not? Gavin, it's been a week. One week! I can't just give up my home."

"This will be your home, or we can find a new place together."

"It's not that easy."

"It is that easy. Whatever it costs to get out of your lease, I'll cover it."

"It's not that. This is new, Gavin. Come on, you can't be serious."

"I'm dead serious. It's easier to have all our stuff at one place. No more 'I should have gone home' or 'I wish I would have packed that.' It will all be right here, where it belongs, where you belong. With me."

"Can we not talk about this right now?" she asks. I can see I've caught her off guard. That's fine. I know she's going to need some time to get to where I am, and I'm okay with that. I know where we're going.

"Sure, baby." I kiss her neck and pull away.

When we finally make it to the office, she seems to have calmed down. Of course, it could be the extra-large coffee and two glazed doughnuts I stopped and picked up for us.

"You know, I can't keep eating like this. I can feel these doughnuts going to my hips as we speak."

"Your hips are perfect."

"You say that now. You won't be thinking that way when I'm big and fat."

"I, for one, can't wait for that to happen," I say, leaning over the console and pressing my lips to hers. My hand lands on her belly. "And you will never be fat."

"I'm not sure we're talking about the same thing," she says, giving me an odd look. Then looking down at my hand on her belly.

"I was talking about eating too much. What were you talking about?"

"Babies, Cass. When we have babies, you're going to be beautiful."

"You feeling all right?" She chuckles.

"Perfect. I'm just tired of holding back from what I want. You and a life with you is what I want." One more kiss and I climb out of the truck. When I reach her side of the truck, she's still sitting there with her mouth hanging open. "You know you should probably close your mouth. You can catch a fly like that." I laugh, holding my hand out for her to help her out of the truck.

She takes my offered hand and climbs out. "My mom used to say that," she says softly.

I close the door and walk us to the elevator, giving her time to work through her feelings. I know she misses her mom like crazy. When the doors close, she seems to snap out of it.

"Babies, Gav?" she questions. Her voice is soft like she's afraid to ask.

"You do want kids, don't you?" I ask her.

She nods. "This is so new. You're talking about moving in together and now babies. We need to slow this train down a little."

The elevator doors slide open, and she walks out. I follow her to her office, walking in behind her and shutting the door. I know the other guys aren't here yet. We're not meeting for another thirty minutes, but just in case. "Is this that new for you, Cass? You and me, in your mind…" I step toward her, placing my hand over her heart. "…in here, are we really new?"

"No."

"You know it's not for me. I've wanted you for longer than I can remember. Life is too short. You of all people know that. I don't want to waste one fucking minute of my time with you holding out because society might look at it as too soon. I know what I feel. I know who my heart beats for. I want it all, baby. As soon as I can get you on board, I want it all."

"Gavin, I—" She closes her mouth when I place my fingers to her lips.

"I'll get you there," I say, leaning in and placing a kiss on her forehead. "Now, get to work, woman. Stop harassing the boss." I wink at her, turn, and stroll out of her office.

CHAPTER 22

DESPITE BEING PREPARED WITH MY laptop and all of my notes in hand, I'm nervous as I sit at my desk and watch the clock. Five more minutes. Five minutes until my first meeting since Gavin and I became official. The guys are great, and good with us dating—they've all told me so last week when they stopped by—but I'm still nervous. My palms are sweating, and I can't stop my knees from bouncing up and down. Watching the clock is making it worse, but I can't seem to stop. I don't want to be too early, or late. I don't want it to look like I'm trying too hard, but then I don't want to seem like I'm slacking on my job now that Gavin and I are an item.

Four minutes.

No longer able to take it, I stand, take a deep breath, and walk down the hall to the conference room. It's empty, and I heave a sigh of relief. I take my usual seat at the back of the table and open my laptop. It's not that we have assigned seating, but it just works out that way. The guys usually sit at the head of the table, and I sit near the back. Taking notes and chiming in when needed.

"Morning." Cole strolls in with a smile on his face. His long hair is pulled back in his signature man bun.

INSISTENT

"Good morning," I say, just as I always do. So far so good. Kacen and Tristan arrive next, all of them taking their usual seats. We share smiles and good morning greetings as well. It's not until Gavin comes waltzing in that my anxiety reaches a high note. Gavin never does what I expect. Instead of taking his seat, he moves down the table and pulls the chair out next to mine. "What are you doing?" I hiss at him.

He gives me a look that tells me I know damn well what he's doing. I chance a look at the other end of the table out of the corner of my eye, and the guys are grinning like fools.

"I like this new development," Cole says, pointing to Gavin and me.

"Me, too." Gavin throws his arm over my shoulder.

"Okay, look." I roll my chair away from his, and his arm falls from my shoulder. "When we're here, I'm Cassidy, your employee. I don't want special treatment, or perks because Gavin and I are—" I stop when Gavin speaks up.

"You're mine," he says, the words almost sounding like a growl. "You've been with us for years. Nothing is going to change, but I'll be damned if I'm going to go all fucking day without touching you or kissing you. It's not going to happen, Cass," he says, crossing his arms over his chest.

"Ga—" I'm interrupted again, this time by Kacen.

"He's right, you know. Logan and I went through something similar, and you can't fight it. This is our company, Cassidy. We say what goes here and we're fine with it." He looks over at Cole and Tristan who are already nodding. "Besides, it's not like this is a fling. That shit would not fly, but when it's the real deal, that changes things. We've discussed this, the four of us. Your job is safe here, your career is not in jeopardy, no matter the outcome of your relationship with Gavin."

"You mean the one where she moves in and we make babies?" Gavin asks, smirking.

I drop my head to the table and groan, causing the four of them to crack up laughing. "Is this happening?" I mumble.

I feel his hot breath against my neck, then the touch of his lips against my skin before he whispers, "Yes. Get used to it. Things are just going to get better from here."

"You've got catching up to do," Cole goads him.

"Right?" Tristan agrees. "Kace and I are working on number two."

"See, babe, we've got to catch up," Gavin says. I can tell by the tone of his voice he's serious. He's not just joking around with the guys.

"Can we just get back to the meeting?" I ask.

"Sure we can, when you scoot your cute ass back over here." Gavin reaches out and grabs the armrest of my chair and pulls me next to him. "You may proceed," he says, dropping his arm back over my shoulder.

I sigh, knowing I've lost the battle. It's just something I'm going to have to get used to. "Did you have a chance to look at the video presentation I sent you?" I ask the guys.

"Yes," they all say at the same time.

"We liked them." I turn to look at Gavin. "The crowd loved them. They seem to have a good local following that extends to the surrounding cities of St. Louis."

"I say we bring them here," Kacen suggests. "Let's get them in the studio, see how easy they are to work with and then we can go from there."

"Agreed," Cole chimes in. "We can be choosy, and I choose to not work with asshats. The kids and the girls will be here a lot. I only want to sign bands we trust. I don't care how big they are or how far their following reaches."

Tristan reaches across the table and holds his fist out for Cole to bump. "I think we can all agree to that," Kacen adds.

"Great, so I'll reach out to them and set it up. You think three days?" I ask the group. "Gavin told them we would be in touch already."

"Yeah," they all agree.

"Okay. There was only one other band that really stood out while we were there. I sent those clips to you as well."

"They had a good sound," Gavin tells them. "Rough around the edges. They would need some work, but that's what we want, right? Bands we can help pave the way for in the industry?"

"Yeah," Kacen agrees, then addresses me. "Cassidy, I'm not sure how much you know about why we bought the label. Some of it was a fuck you to Wilson, the other part was so we could slow down. With the wives and kids, touring can be a little much and we'd rather be with our families."

"Yes." I bob my head, already knowing that's why they bought the label.

"We also decided we would be choosy, as Cole said. None of us need the money. We've all invested well. This is to keep up in the industry. Music is in our blood. None of us were ready to give it up completely," Gavin explains. "Who knows, we might tour again, or put out an album without a tour and see what happens. What we do know is that it's time to focus on our families." He winks at me, and even though I try to act as though I'm annoyed, my heart flips over in my chest.

"Right. Okay, I'll go start the process, and I'll send you all an e-mail letting you know when I have everything set up. Anything else?" I ask, closing my laptop and standing.

"That's perfect. Thank you, Cassidy," Kacen says. Tristan and Cole murmur their thanks as well. I step back from the table, grabbing my things and heading to my office. As soon as I step out of the room, Cole starts talking about his new baby boy and how he has to show them pictures from this morning. I wear a grin all the way to my office. No one on the outside would ever believe me that these four badass rockers are really just big old tattooed teddy bears.

CHAPTER 23

GAVIN

A LL DAY LONG I'VE HAD to keep reminding myself to not bother her, that she's busy. Cass takes her work seriously, and I know a sure-fire way to piss her off is to bother her when she's trying to get shit done. I speak from experience. In the past, I would stop in for mundane reasons just for an excuse to talk to her. I could tell the times she was irritated. Instead of walking away, I would tell her how beautiful she was when she was flustered. That led to her telling me that we were boss-employee and that I couldn't say things like that. I never listened. She didn't see what I saw. She didn't see the ways her eyes would light up when I waltzed into her office and took the seat across from her desk. She didn't see the hope in her eyes after every little speech, that hope told me she was saying what she thought she needed to say. She was saying what seemed appropriate, but that's not how she felt. My only regret with Cass is that I didn't think of the trip, for just the two of us sooner. I owe my boys and their wives props for that one. They helped us get to where we are today.

Her being mine.

The guys left a couple of hours ago. I could have as well, but I never do. I stay until she does if I can. Today though, today is altogether different. When she ends her day, and she's ready to go home, it's my home she's coming to. That means I'll sit here as long as it takes for her to feel like she has a handle on her office after being off all last week. I offered to help her, but she waved me off, begging me to let her work. So, that's what I did. I've been sitting here watching YouTube videos of Shattered Heart to familiarize myself with their work. It's overkill for our meeting, but it's good to watch them and get a feel for their stage presence. Sure, I've seen them live, but Cass was there in my arms, and she was more important. It was a bullshit trip anyway. We knew we were interested. They created this need to go to the festival to get us alone. I'll need to step up my game come Christmas time to repay them.

"Hey," Cass says from behind me.

I turn to face her. "Hey, yourself. You all done? Ready to go home?"

"Yes. I think I've got a handle on things. I'm caught up on returning phone calls, and most of my e-mails. I can do the rest tomorrow."

"You kicked ass and took names today." I stand and pull her into my arms.

She chuckles. "I guess so. I don't like to have to do that, but I hate them thinking that the label or you all are not responding to them."

"Logan fielded some calls last week," I remind her.

"I know she did, and I appreciate that, but that's not her job."

That makes me laugh. "Yeah, it kind of is. She and Stacy share that position. You are Soul Records not Soul Serenade."

"I know that, but they have the kids, and normally it's not an issue. Things are slow around here. The interns are motivated and do great work with the fan club. I just have to oversee it. I don't mind giving them more time with the kids."

"That works for now, but you're going to want that time too," I tell her.

Her eyes go wide and then soften. "Gavin, that's way off."

"Is it?" I ask, nuzzling her neck.

"I'm hungry," she declares, changing the subject. She also knows that there is nothing I won't give her.

"Let's get you home and get you fed." By home, I mean, my place, but she knows that. I had her pack enough clothes to last her a few days for both work and leisure. Last night she tried to go home, but I begged her not to. Yeah, begged. I'm not above that to have her in my bed every night. Instead, I drove her to her place to grab more of her stuff. I cleared her some drawers and half the closet is hers for the taking. Her stuff looks good mingled with mine.

"What are you thinking for dinner?" she asks as we pull up to my condo.

"I make this cheeseburger potato casserole thing. It's good," I tell her.

"Sounds interesting."

"Trust me, it's delicious."

She laughs, and the sound washes over me. I love it. Live for it. "Come on." I grab the keys from the ignition and climb out of my truck. Cass meets me in the front, her purse and work bag thrown over her shoulder. I take them from her, even though she protests, and reach for her hand. Cassidy takes care of everyone else, worries about all of us, her mom, but no one has taken care of her. I've tried to do it from afar, but I'm no longer at arm's length. She's going to have to get used to the fact that looking out for her is my job now. One that I take very seriously.

"Let me change and I'll help you cook."

"Sounds good, babe." I kiss her temple and take her bags into the living room and place them next to the couch. I know my girl and no way can she go all night without checking and responding to some e-mails. Then I head down the hall to my room to change clothes as well. I walk in just in time to see her pull a faded concert shirt over her head. "Damn, I'm too late," I say, grabbing some gym shorts out of my drawer.

"No funny business, Mr. McIntosh. I'm starving."

"Yes, ma'am." I salute her, then make quick work of shedding my jeans and sliding into my shorts. "Ready?" I hold my hand out for her. Her face softens, and I know it's because she secretly loves the way I always want her around. It's a damn good thing I don't see that changing. Ever.

"So how do we make this cheeseburger deliciousness you're talking about?" she asks.

"We need to peel some potatoes and boil them and brown a pound of hamburger. Which would you prefer, my lady?" I ask her, all proper and shit, making her laugh.

"I can do either. Whichever you prefer not to do."

"How are you at peeling potatoes?"

INSISTENT

"Why, I'm the master of course," she teases.

I snake an arm around her waist and kiss her quickly. "I can do it, but I suck balls at it. You peel the taters and I'll work on everything else."

"Taters?" She laughs. "Your southern is showing through, Mr. Rock Star."

I flash her a grin. I'm proud of my country roots. Just because we sing rock music doesn't mean I'm not still a country boy at heart. Hell, I love country music. It's just not our sound, not what we wanted to do.

We spend the next thirty minutes talking, laughing, and cooking. It's domestic as hell and I love every fucking minute of it. She was here last week, but we spent most of our time with her mom, even though she didn't know us. Cass wanted to be there, so that's where we were. We did takeout or just quick sandwiches here at my place. This is the first true meal we've made together. I'm thirty minutes in, and I know this is what I want for the rest of my life.

"Now what do we do?" she asks, watching me drain the water from the potatoes.

"Now, we add these to that casserole dish." I pour them in and place the strainer in the sink. "Then we add the hamburger, some Velveeta cheese, some salt and pepper, a little milk, and bake it just long enough for the cheese to get nice and gooey."

"Who came up with this?" she asks, watching me finish our dinner.

I shrug. "Not sure. My mom used to make it when I was a kid. Not sure if she made it up or if it's some ancient McIntosh masterpiece. What I do know is that it's damn good. We eat it with bread and butter and applesauce. Well, my dad used to eat it with cottage cheese instead, but fuck that. I cannot eat cottage cheese."

She places her hand over her chest and gasps. "Gavin, that's a deal breaker for me. I love cottage cheese," she says, trying to fight her smile.

She's fucking with me. "Baby, I'll buy you all the damn cottage cheese you can eat."

She cracks up laughing. "I hate it." She grimaces. "I can't get past the look. I've actually never tried it, but I don't plan on ever trying it either." She shudders as if it physically makes her sick at the thought.

"Never say never," I say, sliding the casserole into the oven. I turn to where she's leaning against the counter and cage her in, my arms braced on the counter. "What happens when you're pregnant, and you crave

124

it?" I ask, kissing her neck.

"Won't happen," she assures me.

"That's what Stacy said about avocados, and she ate the shit out of them while she was pregnant. Cole said he had to make sure they had them in the fridge at all times."

"That's another thing that's hard to get used to. The four of you gossip and yack like a bunch of women. What would your fan girls think if they heard you all talking about pregnancy cravings?" she asks.

"Don't give a fuck, and chances are they'll never hear it. We keep our family lives personal. Sure, they know we're married, have kids, or what not, but the details are private. Well, except for Cole and Stacy. He brought her up on stage."

"I remember that." She laughs.

"Is that what you want? For me to publicly tell the world how much I love you?"

"No," she says quickly. "I just want you." Her voice is soft.

"So, you're going to move in then?" I ask her.

"Gavin," she sighs.

"Cassidy," I mock her. "Don't think about society, or what you think is the right amount of time. Think about us, how long we've been dancing around this. Think about what's going to make your heart happy. Now—" I kiss the corner of her mouth. "—tell me what you want to say."

"Yes," she breathes.

I can't help it. I'm grinning like a fucking loon. "That's all that matters, Cassidy, is being happy. Life is short, baby. I want to spend it with you. I want all of it. The marriage, the house, the babies, the dog you've always wanted, it's our future. I'll see to it."

"Why are you so insistent that we do this now, this fast?" Her eyebrows furrow as if she's trying to work out a puzzle.

"I love you. I see my brothers and their families, and I want that. When Zach was born…" I swallow hard. "When Zach was born, I realized that no matter how much money you have or fame, none of it matters unless you have someone to share it with. I mean, how amazing is it that love created that tiny little man, a piece of both of them? I held Drew when he was born, but with Zach, it was so different. I had to watch him fight for his life while his mommy did, too. I had to watch Tristan be torn in two over being with each of them. I spent days just sitting next to Zach talking to him, so he knew he wasn't alone, so Tristan could be with Lauren. I watched him grow stronger and bigger each day right before my eyes. I want that with you. I want a little girl with your crazy curls and big blue eyes. I want to watch our baby grow inside of you. I know it sounds crazy, but life is short, and I don't want to wait a second longer to start living it. With you," I say, cupping her cheek. "My heart is yours, Cass." I kiss her deeply.

When I pull back, her eyes are glassy. "You sure you want to share your bed with me?" she asks.

My heart stutters in my chest. "Consider it yours, and you can share it with me," I say.

"My lease is up next month," she confesses.

"What are you saying, Cass?" I pull back and stand to my full height. Placing my finger under her chin, I lift her gaze to mine. "I need to hear you say it."

She braces her hands behind her on the counter and hops up to sit there, crossing her legs. "I'm allowed to do this since I live here now, right?" she asks, smiling.

"Cassidy," I warn her. She's fucking with me. "I need to hear you say it, baby." I stand with my hands at my sides. I want nothing more than to kiss it out of her, but this has to be on her.

"I have a month to get all my stuff moved in. You sure you're ready for that?"

"Cassidy," I growl.

She laughs, a smile lighting her face. "I'm moving in, Gav. You and me." She reaches out, grabs my shirt, and pulls me to her. "We're starting with this. We can see how it goes and talk about the other stuff later."

"Marriage and babies," I say, kissing her nose.

"Yeah," she agrees.

My lips connect with hers, and I try to show her how much this means to me, how much *she* means to me. "I love you, Cass," I murmur against her lips.

"I love you, too."

The timer on the oven dings and I pull away. It's time to feed my girl.

I work on pulling dinner out of the oven and making us plates while Cass pours us a couple of waters. My night was already great because she was here and I knew that I was going to get to fall asleep with her in my arms. It just became a whole hell of a lot better. She's never leaving.

CHAPTER 24

M Y EYES ARE CLOSED BUT I'm awake. I'm basking in the feeling of being tucked in close to Gavin's warm body. But there is a slither of worry still finding its way into my mind. What if he changes his mind? I try to block that one question out, no real idea where it comes from other than having to rely on myself for such a long time. But when I feel his lips kiss my bare shoulder, I can't fight my grin.

"Morning," his deep, sexy voice murmurs.

"How did you know I was awake?" I ask over my shoulder.

"I can hear you thinking. Go ahead and ask me."

"It's a big step."

"It is," he agrees. "One that we're taking together." He kisses my shoulder one more time before climbing out of bed. "Shower. I'll make us some breakfast."

"You're not showering with me?"

"Nope. If I do, we'll never get to the office. You said you have a 9:00 a.m. conference call with Shattered Heart to finalize their visit. It's eight now."

"Shit!" I jump out of bed and rush to the shower. I hear Gavin's deep laugh as I start the water. I rush through my shower and quickly towel off. I'm running my fingers through my wet curls, adding mousse when Gavin walks in carrying a plate.

"It's not gourmet, but you can eat it while you're getting ready." He sets the plate with a bagel and cream cheese on the counter, kisses my shoulder, kicks out of his shorts, and climbs into the shower.

We make it out of the house with just enough time to get to the office a few minutes before nine as long as we don't hit traffic.

"Relax, Cass. They need us, we don't need them. If you're a few minutes late, you can blame it on technical difficulties."

He's right, but I hate being late. Sitting back in the seat, I close my eyes and calm myself down. I also hate rushing. I feel like it sets a hectic tone for the rest of the day. When Gavin's phone rings through the speakers in the truck, he answers it. "Hey, T," he greets Tristan. "You're on speaker with Cass," he informs him.

"Morning," Tristan chirps. "I just wanted to tell you that the place next to mine just went on the market."

"The white brick?" Gavin asks with excitement in his voice. "The one with the huge-ass pool and the grado in the back?" he asks.

"That's the one. I just drove past the sign."

"Go back," Gavin tells him. "Get the number. Better yet, grab the sign, too." He laughs.

"I thought you might say that. Already done," Tristan tells him. "You headed into the office?" he asks.

"Yeah, Cass has a call to make or I'd turn around."

"I'll be there soon. You can then call the realtor."

"Thanks, man." He ends the call and reaches over for my hand. "Do you know which house he's talking about?" he asks me.

"Not really. I know that all the homes there are gorgeous."

"They are. We all spent a lot of time at Kacen's, and then Cole and Stacy bought their place next to his. You know Tristan and Lauren are across the street, and this house, it's the one I've always admired. Not only would that put us with our closest friends, but this place is... you just need to see it. While you're on your call, I'm going to call the realtor and set up a time. What else is on your schedule for today?"

"Nothing pressing but, Gavin, I can't just leave work to look at a house. I was off all last week," I tell him.

"Sure, you can. It won't take us long." He squeezes my hand. "This could be our forever home, Cass. It's all coming together, baby. What would be even better if we can move in right away. Together." He smiles over at me as we pull into the underground parking garage of the label.

"Gavin," I sigh.

"I'll help you do whatever you need to get caught up on. I'll make dinner, so you can work tonight, whatever it takes. I need you to go with me, and we have to go today. No way am I letting this house sell out from under us before we have our shot."

"What if we hate it?"

"If you hate it, we keep looking."

"You can't not buy a house because I don't like it. It's your money, Gavin."

"And you're my future." With that, he climbs out of the truck.

His words have rendered me speechless. This is all really happening. It's fast, but damn if I can keep the smile from pulling at my lips. I also can't control the way my heart races when he says things like that. I want this with him even though I'm scared, but how can I not fall under the spell of what the future holds when he's so excited about it?

"Cass." His voice brings me out of my thoughts.

Looking up, I see him standing with the truck door open, waiting to help me down. "You okay?" he asks.

"Come here." I motion with my finger, and he steps into me. "I love you." I kiss him quickly before pushing him back so I can climb out of his truck. "I'll go with you," I say when we're in the elevator. His reply is to lift our joined hands and kiss my knuckles.

Rushing off the elevator to my office, I set up my laptop and prepare for the conference call. I have three minutes to spare and sigh with relief. Gavin goes to their offices. I'm assuming to call the realtor. Excitement bubbles up inside of me. I can't believe that I agreed to move in with him last night and now, today, we're going to look at a house. A house in a private, gated community no less. How is this my life?

The call with Shattered Heart is what it was meant to be, which is productive. The guys have this weekend open, but gigs after that for the next six weeks. They all have day jobs but agreed they could get Friday off. We planned for them to fly in Friday and out on Sunday. I end the call, letting them know I would e-mail them the flight and room information later today. Normally it would be right after, but Gavin is standing in the doorway of my office listening in, waiting for me to end the call.

"I'll be in touch later today," I inform them one more time.

"Thanks, doll," one of them says.

I don't reply to that comment, but Gavin's eyes go wide. That's what I get for using the speakerphone. It's hard to remember my super hot boyfriend is a little overprotective.

"Doll?" he asks.

"Oh, hush, it's nothing. Did you get a hold of the realtor?"

"I did. He's there waiting for us. I told him we'd be there in half an hour. You ready?"

"Yes." I smile and stand from my desk. Grabbing my purse and phone, I leave everything else, knowing we'll be back later.

CHAPTER 25

W HEN WE PULL UP TO the house, I feel it. This is it. I know she's going to love it as much as I do. I've never stepped foot on the inside, never even seen a picture. The images were not up online yet. The realtor said he just placed the sign this morning. Even with never having seen it, I know this is the house we're going to raise our family in.

The community is private and gated. The street houses only four homes. This one and those of my bandmates, my brothers, and their families. We would have this entire road for us, for our kids to run and play. I can see it all now. I've changed over the last couple of years, even more so when Zach was born.

"Ready?" I ask Cassidy. She's staring out the front window of my truck, her eyes wide.

"Wow," she breathes. "I guess I never really paid too much attention to this place. I've been to each of the other's houses more times than I can count, but never paid this one a bit of attention."

"It's the best one." I wink and climb out of the truck. She meets me in the front, and we head up the bricked walkway. The realtor, Tom, is waiting for us on the front porch.

"Mr. McIntosh, I presume." He holds his hand out for me, and I shake it.

"Yes, this is my Cassidy," I introduce her. She shakes his hand as well, exchanging pleasantries. I expect nothing less from her. She's always polite.

"This place is beautiful," she gushes as we walk into the foyer.

Tom rattles off the square footage, details about granite and tile, and a host of other things that I block out. "Feel free to have a look around. It's available for immediate occupancy. As you can see, the owners have moved out."

"Let's start upstairs," I say to Cass, guiding us toward the grand circular staircase.

"Wow," she says again when we reach the top of the stairs. There are six doors and an open living area. "How many bedrooms is this?"

"Seven," I tell her. We make our way through each room that just so happens to have its own bathroom.

"This is unreal," she breathes as we make our way through the rooms, then back down the staircase.

"Let's go find the master." Her hand still in mine, we make our way to the bottom level. There is a huge living room, dining room, and an additional family room. Off the family area, there's a hall that leads us to the master bedroom. When I push open the double doors, her breath hitches and I smile. Yeah, this is our place.

"Gavin, this is…." Her voice trails off as she spins in a circle, head tilted to the ceiling as she looks at the molding and lighting.

"Let's go check out the bathroom." We open a door that turns out to be a huge walk-in closet. "Think this is big enough for all of our stuff?" I ask her.

"Most definitely," she agrees.

The next door we open is another closet the same size as the one before. "Looks like we won't have to share," I say, stepping back so she can get a better look. She peeks her head in and laughs.

The third door opens to a smaller room. "This must be the private sitting room."

"With a house this size, do you really need a sitting room?" she asks.

"Maybe they liked to watch TV naked and didn't want the kids to see," I suggest, making her laugh again.

The next door opens to a huge bathroom. The walk-in shower has to be at least seven feet long and just as wide. There's a huge claw foot tub, bigger than any I've ever seen, that sits in the corner of the shower, all encased in clear glass. "I guess you don't have to worry about sloshing water everywhere."

"They've thought of everything," she agrees.

Double vanities, with a separate seating area for her to do her hair and makeup sit on the adjacent wall. "Come on." I wrap my arm around her waist and lead her back into the hallway. We still need to see the kitchen and the laundry room. Then the basement and the backyard. The pool looks like an oasis from what I've seen from Tristan's place. "You can only see it in the wintertime," I explain, letting her know we will have privacy in the summer. Not that we need it from our friends.

The kitchen is huge and carries on with the white stone that covers the outside complete with black cabinets and white stone backsplash. The black stainless steel appliances, that are really gray in color but called black—at least that's what it said online—look high-tech. A huge island with white and black marble granite on every surface is in the center of the room.

"Can you see us making dinner here?" I ask her.

She laughs. "I'm not sure. This house is… breathtaking."

"Come on, let's go to the basement." Downstairs, we find a finished basement with a theater room, a built-in bar, and kitchen with a living area. Cass is quiet, just taking it all in, and frankly, so am I. I'm picturing us curled up with our kids watching Disney movies and enjoying family get-togethers in the huge living area upstairs. Making our way back upstairs, we head out back, and Cassidy gasps. There's a huge covered patio that leads to another that is not. Under the covered patio, there's an outdoor kitchen. There is stamped concrete that leads to the pool with the grado and the hot tub.

"We'd never have to leave. Who needs a vacation when you have an oasis right in your backyard? Gavin, this place is… like a resort," she says in awe.

I walk up behind her and place my arms around her waist, holding her close. "Over there, there's plenty of yard for our dog and the kids to play. The property is already fenced in," I say, kissing her neck. "Can you see us living here, Cass? Can you see us raising a family here?" I close my eyes and say a silent prayer that she says yes. This is the home

I want for us. It's everything I would build if I was designing from scratch, but the bonus is that the guys are our neighbors, and this is our street. Maybe we can get them to rename it Soul Street or Serenade Drive?

She turns in my arms and looks up at me. "What do you think? Can you see... us here?" she asks hesitantly.

"Before I answer you, let me make one thing clear. It's us. No matter what decision is made, we make it together. It's us from now until I take my last breath, so don't ever hesitate with that again, okay?" I ask, softening a little.

"Can you see us here?" she asks again, this time with more confidence.

"Yes. I can see it."

"Do you want it?"

"Do you?" I counter.

She closes her eyes and buries her face in my chest. I can feel her body shake, and I'm just about to ask her what's wrong when she looks up with a smile so bright, it rivals the sun. "I do, Gavin. I want it. I want us. I want this house. I want everything I know you're thinking and I'm too scared to say. I want that with you," she confesses.

My arms tighten around her, as everything I've imagined in the last hour going from room to room in this house flashes through my mind. "Okay, baby," I say, kissing the top of her head. "Let's go buy our house." Hand-in-hand we walk back inside and find the realtor in the foyer on his phone. "Tom," I greet him. "We'll take it. Full asking price, cash. We want this deal closed so we can move in within the month."

Tom fumbles his phone but catches it and gets himself together. "Yes, sir, Mr. McIntosh. The sellers are motivated. I'm sure even if the deal is not complete, you could move in."

"Make it happen, Tom," I say again, and he nods. "You have my number." With that, Cass and I head back to my truck and toward the office. When we get to the parking garage, I see all the guys are here, which is perfect; I can tell them about the house. Cass tries to let go, to go to her office, but I keep a tight hold on her hand, and we go in search of the guys. We follow the voices upstairs, which tells me either they have the kids or their entire families are with them. As we hit the top of the stairs, all eyes land on us. The guys, their wives, and kids are sitting in the common area.

"Perfect. Everyone's here," I say, taking a seat on the sectional that's open—the one for me and my family. The family I wasn't sure would happen because the girl I loved was fighting it. The same family that's now within reach and we're buying a house to start making the dream a reality. "We bought a house," I blurt. I look over at Tristan. "Hey, neighbor." I wave and he laughs.

"Wait, that place is for sale?" Stacy asks. Cole is beside her with Riley fast asleep on his chest.

"Now that entire street is ours," Lauren chimes in as she rocks Zach in her arms. Tristan has his arm around her, staring down at them in wonder.

"We need to rename the street." Logan laughs. Drew laughs, too, because if his mommy is laughing, he knows it must be funny.

"What are you laughing at?" Kacen picks him up from where he's been playing with trucks on the floor and tickles his side.

"Daddy stop," rings out through the room, along with his giggles, and I can't help but smile.

"I said the same thing. Serenade Drive sounds nice," I add.

"So, when are you moving in?" Lauren asks.

"We told the realtor that we wanted it this month. Cass's lease is up on her condo in a month, and she was moving in with me anyway." I feel her stiffen beside me, no doubt worried about their reaction. She doesn't need to be. "So we thought it would be best to move just the once, both of us into the new place."

"Congratulations!" Logan is up and enveloping Cass into a hug, followed by Lauren, and then Stacy who is moving a little slower than the others having just given birth a few weeks ago.

"It's soon," Cass admits.

"Pfft," Cole comments. "Who gives a fuck about time? You do what makes you happy. If I could have, this one"—he puts his arms back around Stacy when she sits back beside him—"would have been married and pregnant in week one." The group laughs, and I can feel Cass relax even further.

We talk a little more, and the girls make plans to meet up with Cassidy as soon as we have the keys to see the new place. "You okay with that?" she asks me.

INSISTENT

"Cassidy, it's your home, too. Decorate it however you want, paint it whatever color you want. I don't give a fuck as long as when I go to bed at night, you're lying there beside me."

The girls *ooh* and *ahh,* while the guys stay silent. I didn't expect a reply from them. Every one of those fuckers fell just as hard as I did. Some faster. I've been wanting her from a distance for longer than I can remember.

CHAPTER 26

I T'S FRIDAY AFTERNOON AND ALL the gang is here, waiting on Shattered Heart to arrive. I arranged for a car to pick them up at the airport and take them to their hotel, then bring them here. Logan is here as well. She left Drew with Lauren and Zach, so she could come in and help me get everything together. I told her I could handle it, but she insisted. I'm grateful she's here. It's nice to not be the only woman in the sea of men.

"Apparently, they have a manager," I tell the guys and Logan as we sit around the conference table. "They e-mailed me yesterday stating he was coming with them, and they would arrange for him to have a room, that we didn't need to worry about it. Of course, it worked out. I booked them a suite that has a fold out couch. It was more cost effective than four separate rooms," I explain.

"Good call," Logan says. "I would have done the same thing."

Logan and I are a lot alike in that aspect. Just because the guys can afford it doesn't mean they need to be lavish and waste money. Especially with a band that's not even signed yet. Who knows how this meeting will go. They were cocky the night of the festival, but it was obvious they'd had a few beers. I know these four will not put up with that. Gavin and I both relayed that information but felt it was worth a face-to-face anyway.

When the buzzer over the front door alerts us that they've arrived, I stand to go greet them. The underground garage is for us only. That way we always know that when we drive in, it's safe, no matter what time of day or night. It was open to anyone previously, but when the guys bought the label, they changed it. They take the protection of their families very seriously. My heart swells in my chest knowing I'm a part of that now. I hope to be for a very long time.

I round the corner and see Brian, Alan, Scott, and Eric, the members of Shattered Heart. There is a fifth person in the back, but I figure we can meet once we're in the room. "Gentlemen, thanks for coming. How was your flight?" I ask politely.

"Good," one of them speaks up from behind me.

"I hope the room works out for all of you," I say, leading them toward the conference room door. We're just walking through it when one of them speaks up.

"You could come by later and check it out yourself."

My eyes go wide. I know that voice. Apparently, the guys do, too. They all stand, and Gavin rushes to me, grabbing my hand and pulling me behind him. A quick glance beside me and I see Kacen has done the same with Logan.

"First of all, you ever fucking look at her or speak to her like that again, I'll tear your fucking head off."

"What the fuck are you doing here? You're supposed to be in jail," Cole seethes.

Looking over, I see Tristan has a hand on Cole's shoulder, holding him back. Wilson, the bastard who pushed himself on Stacy, the previous owner of Stone Records now Soul Records, stands before us wearing a sleazy grin.

"Cassidy, Logan, you ladies are looking sexy as always," he says, and I hear all four of the guys growl. "Cole, where's that lady of yours?"

Cole lunges for him, but Tristan holds tight.

"Get the fuck out of here," Tristan seethes.

"What in the hell is going on here? What are we missing?" Brian, the lead singer for Shattered Heart, speaks up.

"What's going on is this fucked asshole tried to rape my wife, his ass was thrown in jail for that and a whole host of other things," Cole grits out.

"You what?" Brian turns to Wilson. "You told us you knew them from being in the industry."

"It's not my fault you weren't smart enough to do your homework."

Wilson pulls out a gun and points it at Cole, and I bury my face in Gavin's back. His hand that is still on my hip behind him tightens. Gavin's phone is sticking out of his back pocket. Luckily his broad shoulders shield me. Logan finds my eyes and nods. She, too, is hidden behind Kacen. Making sure the phone is turned to vibrate, I dial 911 and pray they can catch the conversation and they get here fast.

"You," Wilson roars, "you and that stupid bitch. I should have just fucked her. I paid for it regardless."

Anger pitches his voice high. He sounds unhinged, and knowing he has a gun, he's completely batshit crazy. I pray the police get here soon.

"Did you really think I would let you get away with it? Let you get away with ruining my life, buying my label?"

"Fuck you!" Cole sneers.

"We bought this place from the bank. It's not our fault that you're a slimy bastard and lost it all," Tristan seethes.

Gavin and Kacen have been calm, both have a tight grip on each of us. I assume that's the only reason they're not firing off as well.

"You, the four of you and your bitches, you ruined my life." His angry voice is piercing, dangerous.

"Hey, man, why don't you calm down, give me the gun?" This from one of the guys in Shattered Heart.

"Fuck off, get over there," he sneers. "All of you get the fuck over there!" he roars. Footsteps sound across the floor and then his manic laugh. "Looks like I got me a little firing squad," he boasts. "Logan and Cassidy, get your asses out here. Stop hiding," he rants.

"Over my dead fucking body," Gavin says. His voice is deep and menacing.

"Put the fucking gun down, Wilson. Do really want to go back to prison?" Kacen asks him.

"Why the fuck not?" he asks. "My life is ruined. I can't get a job. This is all I know, and you all fucked me over."

"You tried to rape my wife!" Cole booms, causing me to jump. Looking over at Logan, I see she has a tight hold on Kacen's shirt. I can imagine the fear in her eyes is the same vision reflected back at her in mine.

"Put the gun down," Tristan says, his voice threatening.

"Fuck you!" Wilson screams.

When a shot rings out, I fall to my knees, bringing Gavin down with me. I'm holding on to him as if he's a life preserver in the middle of the ocean. Chaos is breaking out with lots of screaming and yelling, another shot rings out, and I cringe, trying to get closer to Gavin. I'm shaking, and tears are running down my face. I don't know what's happening because I'm too scared to look. All I know is that Gavin has a tight hold around me and he keeps whispering that everything is going to be okay.

"Police!" I hear shouted, and then the command for Wilson to put his gun down. Another shot rings out, more screaming, more chaos, and all I can do is hold on to Gavin, praying we get out of this alive, that we all do.

We just agreed to move to the next chapter of our lives and now this. Gavin's words telling me that life is too short races through my mind on a loop. He's right, and I send up a silent prayer that if we make it out of this, no more holding back. I want him, I want everything, and I won't let fear keep me from it.

Life is too short.

"Cass, baby, it's okay. It's over," Gavin whispers.

Over? I try to process what he's saying, but fear has me frozen in place. I keep my head buried in his chest, and my grip on his shirt is tight as I pull myself closer to him.

"They have him, Cass. It's okay, baby. I've got you," he murmurs. His hands stroke gently over my hair, and he alternates between kissing me on the temple and whispering over and over again that it's over. "Let me see those eyes, gorgeous." His voice is low and calm. I listen, and the madness just surrounding us seems to have faded. Slowly, I lift my head and he smiles. "There she is." He cups my face in his big hands. "You good? Are you hurt?"

"No. I'm not hurt, are you? The gun shots… is everyone okay?" I look around. There are some cops talking to the others, but I don't see

Wilson anywhere.

"No one got hurt. He was shooting in the air, crazy motherfucker. They got him. He's in cuffs, and he'll be going back to jail for a long time."

"Everyone's okay?" I ask again, running my eyes over every inch of him, searching for an injury.

"We're all good." He kisses my lips quickly then stands, pulling me up with him. Over the next couple of hours, we each give our statements to the police, and the entire time, Gavin never lets me out of his sight. He has his hand on the small of my back, his arm thrown over my shoulders, his arms wrapped around my waist from behind. Never once does he break the connection between the two of us.

Once the officers clear out, we decide that calling it a day is best. The decision is made to meet back here tomorrow morning. The guys from Shattered Heart apologize over and over, and we tell them it's not their fault. Wilson is an evil man. They were played.

"Ready to go home?" Gavin asks.

Funny how when he says home, I no longer think of my condo but his. "Yeah."

Once we're in his truck, he looks over at me. "I could have lost you today." He tucks a curl behind my ear. "I've never been that scared, Cass."

"I love you." Three little words that don't seem like nearly enough, but I hope he understands what I'm trying to convey.

"Love you, too." He kisses me quickly and then hits the door sensor to drive out of the underground garage.

All I want to do is shower, then curl up in bed with him. I need him close. I need to feel his heartbeat under my palm. I just need him.

CHAPTER 27

I'M DRIVING ON AUTOPILOT. MY grip on Cassidy is firm and unyielding. Today was fucked. Fucking, Wilson, I hope they throw the motherfucking book at him. I'll be calling our attorney. I want to press charges, anything that will stick. I want them to throw it at him. I'm sure the guys will agree.

When I think about how she was in danger, and Logan too, fuck, I want to rip him limb from limb. My grip on the wheel tightens and apparently, so does my grip on Cass.

"Hey." She rubs her hand up my arm. "We're okay," she soothes, knowing exactly what's going through my mind.

Lifting our joined hands to my lips, I kiss her knuckles. I need to get home and I need her in my arms, sooner rather than later. I press the accelerator a little harder. When we pull up in front of my place, I turn off the engine and look over at her. "Wait for me." I rush out of the truck and to her door. She has it open and is waiting, legs turned sideways, waiting for me. Gripping her hips, I place her on the ground. Keeping one arm around her, I close her door and lead us into the house.

As soon as the door is shut and locked, I crush her in my embrace. "I love you, Cass," I whisper.

Her hands thread through my hair as she murmurs that she loves me, too.

"I need to show you, Cass. I need...." My voice trails off when she places her delicate finger over my lips.

"Yes. To whatever it is you need, my answer is yes."

I crush my mouth to hers, my tongue pushing past her lips, swirling and dueling with hers. Tasting her, but it's not enough. Lifting her in my arms, I head upstairs to our bedroom. It stopped being just mine the first night she stayed here. Forevermore, anything of mine will be hers.

I bypass the bed and go straight to the shower. I need to wash away the day, wash away the grime of being in the same room with that psycho. I need to try and wash it away from her. I don't want anything from him to touch her. I can't imagine what Cole is going through right now. I make a mental note to call him, but if I know Cole, he's with his wife and son, doing exactly what I'm doing. Proving to himself that they're fine. Stacy and Riley were not even there, and I know without a doubt that's exactly what he's doing.

Setting Cass on the counter, I pry myself away from her to start the water. When I turn to undress her, she's way ahead of me. She walks to me and pulls at the hem of my T-shirt. I lift my arms and bend down, allowing her to pull it over my head. Her hands run down my chest lovingly, as if she's memorizing every inch of my skin. When she reaches the waistband of my jeans, she makes quick work of the button and zipper and tugs to get them over my hips. They drop to the floor, boxer briefs and all. I step out of them, kicking them to the side.

Without a word, I bend, place my hands on the back of her thighs, and lift. She jumps and wraps her legs around my waist. I step into the shower and let the hot water rain down on us. My face is buried in her neck, and her hands are gripping my hair.

"I'm right here," she whispers.

My grip tightens. Fuck, I can't lose her, not now that she's mine. I finally have her, we're moving forward, and that motherfucker puts her at risk. I kiss her neck, needing to taste her. I need all of my senses wrapped up in nothing but Cassidy.

"I could have lost you." Her words echo my thoughts.

Finally, I lift my head to look at her. "I don't know what I would have done had something happened to you."

"To any of you," she amends. "Our friends, your family, the other band, he put us all in danger," she says quietly.

She's right, I know she is, but I can't get past the part where she could have been hurt. I adjust my hold on her as our skin grows slippery from the hot water raining down on us. My cock is nestled in her heat, and with a gentle push, I slide home, filling her. Her hold on my hair tightens, and a soft moan falls from her lips. My grip is strong, so I know I can move, and she'll be safe, but I just want to remain like this, for just a minute. I just want this feeling to wash over me. She's my home, my everything, and I want to bask in her heat, and in the knowledge we're both home where we belong. Safe.

"Gav?"

I lift my head to look at her. Her eyebrows are furrowed and her eyes full of concern. She has nothing to be worried about. I have her here safe in my arms, that's all I'll ever need. "Marry me?" The words escape my lips before I realize it, but I don't regret it, and I won't take the question back. Her mouth is making a cute little *O* of surprise, but it doesn't stop me from asking again. "Marry me." This time it's less of a question and more of a demand. I need her with me, like this forever.

She opens her mouth, then shuts it again. She starts shaking her head, and I begin to formulate a plan. I need her to be my wife. "Only you," she whispers, a smile forming on her lips.

"I need your words, baby."

"Yes."

I rock my hips and pull out, then push slowly back inside of her. "Yeah?" I ask, sliding out and easing my way back home.

She nods, and this time her smile shines through, and it's blinding. "Yes."

I kiss her. My lips devour hers as I slowly make love to her. I stop rocking my hips and focus on her lips. I trace her bottom lip with my tongue, nipping it with my teeth and then soothing it once again with my tongue. "I love you," I whisper, kissing her slowly as if I have all the time in the world. She lifts herself up, gripping her legs around my waist, and then lowers back down. She repeats this three times before I get the hint. "You need more, baby?"

"Yes," she moans, as I meet her downward thrust with one of my own.

INSISTENT

"That's my new favorite word from you," I say, rocking into her.

"I need more," she says, sapphire eyes blazing.

Who am I to deny my fiancée anything? Taking a few small steps, I push her against the wall and give my girl what she wants. I thrust hard and fast over and over, and in no time, she's gripping my cock; her walls are going crazy, and I'm chasing her orgasm as much as I'm chasing mine.

"Yes," she pants. "Don't stop. Please, don't stop." She clings to my shoulders, digging her nails into my flesh, and I love it.

"Never," I assure her. I'll never stop loving her, or making love to her. Never stop chasing our mutual pleasure. I have the rest of our lives to show her that.

"Gavin!" she screams, and her pussy grips me like a vise. I try to hold off, but it's too much. I release inside of her, giving her everything I've got.

Once we've caught our breath, I lower her to her feet but keep my arms wrapped around her.

"My legs feel like Jell-O," she says with a laugh.

"That means I did my job." I kiss her temple. Reaching for the body wash, I wash every inch of her creamy skin, then her hair. She rinses off and steps out of the shower while I finish up. When I turn off the water, she's standing there, a towel wrapped turban style around her head and one around her body, holding another out for me.

"Thank you, fiancée." I grin.

She just shakes her head and smiles.

"We're doing this, Cass. You're not backing out on me. I got your words, you said yes," I remind her.

"Meh, it was the heat of the moment." She turns and walks out of the bathroom.

Fuck that. I chase after her, picking her up and tossing her on the bed. "Take it back," I warn, poised over her, my hands at her sides.

"And if I don't?" she taunts. That's when I know she's fucking with me.

"I'll have no choice but to do this." I pull on the corner of the towel that's tucked in next to her plump breasts, holding it closed. It opens easily, and I take action, burying my fingers in her sides and tickling her.

She squirms under me, her laughter filling the room.

"G-G-Gav!" she squeals. "S-stop, please," she begs.

I freeze my hands. "Tell me," I say, my hands poised for another attack.

Her sapphire eyes smile up at me. "I love you, fiancé." She smirks.

"Damn right, you do." I lean over her, careful not to crush her, and press my lips to hers. "I love you, too. Now, you get ready for bed. I'll go grab us some food." I kiss her one more time and head to the kitchen.

"Gavin!" she yells. I turn to look at her. "You're naked," she says, her cheeks heating as she points to my nakedness that's now saluting her from our little game.

"And I expect you to be when I get back. I need you close, nothing between us tonight." With that, I turn and leave her.

I make us a couple of lunchmeat sandwiches, grab a bag of chips, and two bottles of water, and head back to the room. Cass is in bed, a sheet pulled up over her naked breasts, and her blonde curls are in a wet knot on top of her head. I set the food in the middle of the bed, then crawl in beside her. I know I'm grinning like a fool, but I couldn't give a fuck less. I have a lifetime of midnight snacks with her. I didn't plan to propose this way. I wanted to use the video to make it special for her, but the words presented themselves, and even though I didn't plan it, I want it more than anything. Want her. I'll just plan something special when I give Cass her ring. The one that I'm going out tomorrow to purchase. My girl needs a symbol of my love for her. Sooner rather than later.

CHAPTER 28

WAKE TO GAVIN SITTING on the edge of the bed. "Hey," I say groggily.

"Hey, beautiful." He leans in and presses a kiss to my forehead.

"What time is it?"

"Just after eight."

"Why are you up and dressed?"

"Kace called early. We're going to meet with Shattered Heart, and all the wives and kids are going to Stacy's. She's pretty shaken about yesterday."

"Let me get ready and I'll go in with you."

"Actually, we're just going to jam with them today, get a feel for their talent and how they vibe with each other. I was going to drop you off at Cole and Stacy's on my way."

"Okay, yeah. I can do that. Are you sure they won't mind?" I ask.

He pulls his phone out of his pocket and taps the screen. It's a text from Logan. I lean in closer to see the screen.

> **Logan:** Bring Cassidy to us. We are going to rally around Stacy today.

I smile. "I'll get ready." I throw the sheet off me, exposing my naked body to him.

"I'll be downstairs." His eyes roam over me. "I can't stay here and us not be late." He smacks my ass as he stands and strolls out the door.

I jump out of bed and rush to the bathroom. While the shower is heating, I brush my teeth. I have to take another quick one because curly hair is not my friend when I go to bed with it wet and tied in a knot on the top of my head.

I race through putting product in my hair and pull out my hairdryer and diffuser from under the sink. I get the dampness out of my hair and decide to let it air-dry the rest of the way. After throwing on some shorts, a tank, and flip-flops, I find Gavin in the kitchen.

"Ready?" he asks, raking his eyes over me.

"Yep. Maybe we should stop and get breakfast. Some muffins or something?"

"We can do that," he says, reaching for my hand. Grabbing my purse and phone from the counter, I take his offered hand and let him lead me out to his truck.

When we get to Cole and Stacy's, Gavin carries in the box of muffins, even though I tell him I can get it.

"I know you can," he says as we reach the front steps. "I can also do it for you. Get used to it, Cass." He leans in and presses his lips to mine, and that's how Lauren finds us with Zach on her hip.

"Good morning, you two." She smiles.

Gavin hands her the muffins that I couldn't carry and takes Zach from her arms. "Hey, buddy," he says, offering the baby his finger.

I watch them, and my heart swells. This incredible man is mine, all mine. I can't believe this is where we are, from months and months of denying and fighting it, to moving in together, to buying a house, and now getting married. I feel like if I blink, I'll miss something that's important.

I don't want to blink.

His pocket vibrates and he groans. "I gotta go, bud, but I'll be back later to get my girl," he tells Zach. He turns to me and nods toward the adorable little boy in his arms, and I reach for him. Lauren left us here in the foyer to take the muffins into the kitchen. "We need one of those," he says, kissing me quickly. "I'll be back as soon as I can. Love you." He gives my hip a gentle squeeze.

"Love you, too. Be safe," I add, because yesterday is still at the forefront of my mind.

"You know it. We have a wedding to plan," he says, and there is a loud gasp from behind me. He winks and strolls out the front door.

I hadn't decided if I was going to tell them. Not because I thought they wouldn't be on board, but I wanted it for me, just for a while, and with everything going on with Stacy and Wilson, I didn't want to take away from that. I'm here for her, to support her—not steal the show. Slowly I turn and see Stacy with a huge-ass smile on her face.

"Did I hear that right?"

I nod. "I'm sorry. I know you have a lot going on. I was going to wait to say something."

"What?" she screeches. "This is awesome. This is exactly what I need. Wilson is a bastard, and I know he's behind bars again, where he belongs. We have to keep living, and this is living at its best. Not to mention that we've been rallying for the two of you for months now." She smirks.

Zach coos and I look down at him. "You hear that, little man? They were all voting against me," I coo right back.

"The opposite," Stacy says. "We wanted you with him. We've seen it. Once we put the idea in our husbands' heads, they were on board to help us make it happen." She claps her hands. "Come on, we have to tell the others." She skips off into the living room, moving much faster than I would have thought for a woman who just gave birth three weeks ago, but you can't even tell she was pregnant. She's one of those. So far, so are Lauren and Logan, too. These ladies are like superheroes.

I follow after her, then settle onto the couch with Zach. Looking over at Stacy, I see she's practically bouncing in her seat. "Should you be bouncing around like that?" I tease her.

She sticks her tongue out at me. "Speak," she orders and laughs. I must hesitate too long for her. "Cassidy has something to tell us." She grins.

"Gavin and I are buying the house," I tell them. I'm sure they already know this, but I'm messing with Stacy.

"That's what we heard," Lauren pipes up. "Did they accept your offer?"

"They did," Stacy answers for me. "They move in next week."

I gape at her, but then I remember our men chat more than women, and of course they tell their wives. Gavin got the call the day we put our offer in that we could close next week. I guess when you pay cash, that changes the game. You don't have to wait for inspections or appraisals. Gavin did schedule an inspection though, but informed me and the realtor that regardless of what was discovered, we would still buy the house. I believe his exact words were, "I don't care if we have to tear the damn thing down, we're buying it." What he didn't say was that he wanted to live there. The house is amazing, but even more important is its location to his family. His band of brothers.

"And," Stacy prompts me.

"Anndd," I drag out the word. "Oh, yeah, we're getting married." I shrug like it's no big deal. Shrieks surround me, babies startle, and I'm engulfed in hugs. Well, as much as they can with baby Zach in my arms.

"Congratulations," Logan says.

"When did this happen?" Lauren asks.

"We need details," Stacy says, finally settling into her seat.

I smile at my friends. I've been so wrapped up in caring for Mom and worrying about letting her down and avoiding Gavin, that I missed the fact that we are indeed friends. I tell them about last night, the shower, all of it. "Life's short," I say finally.

"Wow." Lauren grins. "Gav has good taste."

"Yes. Yes, he does," I agree.

"So, when is this going down?" Stacy asks.

"Yeah, what can we do to help?" Logan asks.

My eyes fill with tears. "I'm not sure, to be honest. I've never really thought about it."

"Well, let me tell you," Lauren says, taking a drink of her water bottle before she continues, "these guys, they love hard and fast, and he's going to want your name changed sooner rather than later." Stacy and Logan agree with her.

"I guess I need to talk to Gavin, so we can figure it out."

Stacy laughs. "Trust me, he's going to tell you that he doesn't care what you want, just that he wants it soon."

"That's basically what we all got," Stacy says. "You remember that, right? You've been there through it all. Now you're on the receiving end." She smirks.

"Well, if you are planning something big, for the sake of full disclosure, I guess I need to tell you I'm pregnant," Logan blurts.

This time the congratulations and hugs are hers. I can't help but feel excitement bubble up inside. That's going to be me, very soon if Gavin has his way. To be honest, I want it, too. Even though Mom might not know it's her grandchild, I'd love for her to be around to meet him or her.

"So, what are you thinking?" Lauren asks.

"Honestly, I don't really care, but I would like for my mom to be there. She might not know I'm her daughter, but there is a part of me that hopes deep down she knows." I stop before I start bawling my eyes out.

"We'll make it happen," Logan assures me. "You think about it, decide for sure what you want, and we'll make it happen."

"Now." Stacy claps her hands. "Let's eat those muffins your man brought in this morning."

"What?" Lauren laughs. "You've been hiding muffins?"

"Not me." I point to Stacy. "She needed the latest." I laugh.

"Damn right." Her face grows serious. "Thank you, I needed this today. I need time with my girls."

We move to the kitchen and put a dent in the box of muffins. The whole time I'm holding a slumbering baby boy in my arms. I'm excited for this next adventure, and Gavin's not going to get a fight from me. I'm ready to marry him, to have his babies. Each day we're reminded that we don't know how much time we have, so living it is all we can do. I plan to do just that, as Cassidy McIntosh.

CHAPTER 29

 GAVIN

A S SOON AS I DROPPED Cass off at Cole and Stacy's, I headed to meet the guys, just not at the studio. Instead, I met them at the jewelers. I need to buy Cass a ring, and my brothers who have been there before offered to come along for the ride when I asked them who they used.

When I pull into the lot, the three of them are standing out front. "How long have you been waiting?" I ask them.

"Not long. We rode together. We must have just missed you at the house," Cole says.

"You ready for this?" Tristan asks.

"Yes."

"No second thoughts?" Kacen asks.

"What the…?" I whip my head around to tell him what he can do with his second thoughts to find him laughing. "Nice." I chuckle.

"Let's get your girl a ring," Cole says, knocking on the door.

The store doesn't open until eleven, but one of the guys made a call, and here we are, an hour before opening. We'll have the place to ourselves. I'm not worried about finding a ring as I'll know when I see it. At least I hope I will.

"Gentlemen," an older man greets us.

"Thanks for opening up early," I say, shaking his offered hand. "Gavin," I add, remembering my manners.

"The groom I presume." He chuckles.

"Yes, sir," I say proudly. Damn right is what I wanted to say, but I hold my tongue and try to keep it professional.

"Do you know what you are looking for? Ideas?" he asks.

"No, I was hoping to just take a look around. I'm hoping that something pops out to me."

"It usually does. I have a selection that we don't keep in the cases. Highest quality of stones with color and clarity. If you want to follow me to the back, I'd be happy to show you."

With a nod, the four of us follow him to a conference room. Taking a seat around the table, he scoots a black display case toward me. My palms are sweating; this is finally happening. I'm not nervous, but I am excited as fuck that she's mine. That she's going to be my wife.

My eyes scan the display. There must be a hundred rings, and I give each one my full attention, trying to envision it on Cass's hand. The guys are silent beside me, letting me do my thing. When I get about halfway through, I see it. "This one." I point to the ring.

"Ah," he says, pulling the ring out of the case and handing it to me. "This is an excellent choice. It's simple, yet stunning at the same time. What you're looking at is a three-carat center stone princess cut. Round diamonds in a total half carat per side and up the band." He rattles on about the cut and color, clarity, but I tune him out. This is the one. I can't wait to see this on her hand every day for the rest of our lives. "A total of four carats," he says, tugging me out of my thoughts.

"I'll take it." Reaching into my pocket, I pull out a small silver band that Cass wears on the opposite hand, but same finger. "This is her size."

"Nice." Cole nods, impressed.

"I swiped it from the nightstand this morning. She was in such a rush to get to your place, she didn't mention not being able to find it." That was all a part of my plan. It's the reason I snuck out of bed to get ready. I wanted her to be rushing; she hates to keep people waiting. It was my hope that she wouldn't notice and if she did, she wouldn't stop to look for it, assuming it fell onto the floor. My plan worked and here we are.

"Six," he says, handing it back to me. "This is also a six, so you can take it with you today," he informs me. "If you want."

I nod. "I want." I thought I would have to wait, but the stars seem to be aligning in my favor. I hand him my black Am Ex, and he runs the transaction. I didn't ask how much it costs and I don't care. It's perfect, and I can't wait to slide it on her finger.

"So, where to now?" Tristan asks once we leave the jewelry store. I have one hand in my pocket, clutching the small velvet box in my hand.

"Shattered Heart is meeting us at the studio," Kacen reminds him.

"Damn, I thought that was just a ploy."

"It was in a way, but we still have to meet with them. Just a quick jam session."

"Meet you guys there," I say, heading toward my truck.

"I'll ride with you," Tristan says, climbing in the passenger seat. Cole and Kacen climb in Cole's truck. "How are you going to do it?" he asks once we're on the road and headed to the label.

"Not sure. I mean, I already asked her and she said yes, but I have this video." I grab my phone and unlock it. "It's the last video I recorded," I say, handing him my phone. Tristan taps on the screen and then I hear my voice and that of Margaret's fill the car.

"Damn," Tristan mutters once the video ends.

"Yeah, I want to show her that." I nod toward my phone before looking back at the road. "Then give her the ring."

"Expect tears, brother," he warns.

"Yeah," I agree. I hate to see her cry, but I know they will be sad and happy tears combined. She needs to see the video. She's no longer fighting this love that we have, but I know she doubts herself at times. I'm hoping this will end that. That she can know that her mom is with her, even when she's not, and she can let herself live in the moment.

Three hours later, we're shaking hands with Brian, Alan, Scott, and Eric. Shattered Heart has a handshake deal to sign with Soul Records. They are crazy talented and remind me a lot of us in the early days.

"Our attorney will send over a contract next week. Take your time, have yours look it over. If you don't have one, feel free to reach out to ours. He's fair and will explain anything you're not sure about. No hidden agendas," Kacen tells them. "We just want to make music. It's in our blood. We have wives and families and touring is not what we want right now, but we can help others reach that goal."

"Go, enjoy Nashville for a night. You have your flight info for tomorrow?" I ask, because I know that Cass will ask me and I need her full attention.

"Yeah. Cassidy—" Brian starts, but I interrupt him.

"My fiancée," I say, smiling.

"—she made sure we had what we needed," he finishes.

"Great. You'll have the contract next week. Stay out of trouble, and don't worry about a manager. That's something we can do for you. Feel free to seek out advice from our attorneys if you don't have your own throughout the process," Kacen reminds them.

"Thank you," Eric says.

"We won't disappoint you," Scott adds.

"We can't thank you enough," Alan chimes in.

"We look forward to it," Brain says. He reminds me a lot of Kace.

He founded the band and is somewhat the leader, just like us. I have a really good feeling about this. They're great guys, but I'm ready for them to be gone. I have a girl to go see. Once they finally walk out the door, I rush to lock up behind them, making the guys laugh.

"Dinner at my place," Cole says, reading his phone. "Our wives have it under control is what I'm told." He smiles.

Wives. She's not mine yet, but she will be and having him refer to her as so does something to me. The sweaty palms are back, but again it has nothing to do with nerves; it's pure adrenaline. I hope she doesn't make me wait long. I can't wait for her to be mine, legally. She's already mine, but not in the eyes of the law. We're about to change that.

When we get to Cole's and walk through the front door, we hear feminine laughter along with that of the kids. Like lost puppies, we follow the sound, and we find all four women, and all three kids, sitting in the living room with pizza boxes spread out. Drew is dancing to the music that plays in the background. They're cheering him on and he's eating it up. Can't say I blame him. Kace scoops him up in his arms and tickles him before they settle on the loveseat next to Logan. Kace kisses her hello and Drew mimics his dad.

Tristan takes Zach from Lauren and nuzzles him before kissing her hello and sitting on the floor between her legs. He better enjoy it while he can; I plan to steal my little bud before the night is over. All of them in fact. Uncle Gavin needs a fix of his nephews.

Cole beelines for Stacy and sits next to her. I watch as he whispers in her ear; I'm sure checking on how she's feeling. My eyes search the room and land on Cass. My beautiful girl is sitting on the chaise lounge with baby Riley in her arms. She's staring down at him, looking content as hell, and my heart stutters in my chest. I can't wait to see her grow with our baby. Needing to be next to her, I slide in behind her on the lounge and kiss her neck. "We need one," I whisper. I want to align my body with hers, but I can't chance her feeling the ring in my pocket. Plus, Drew doesn't need to see that. The others can look away. I've witnessed the same with them and their wives.

"We do," she agrees, shocking the hell out of me.

"Yeah?" I ask.

"Yeah. He's such a good baby. They all are." She looks over her shoulder at me.

"Tell me when, Cass. You can stop taking your pills tonight as far as I'm concerned."

"Okay," she agrees.

I squeeze her hip. "Baby, are you listening to me?" No way did she agree to tossing her pills. Not that easily.

She giggles. "I heard you, Gav."

"No more pills?" I ask, my lips next to her ear.

"No more," she whispers back.

"Sorry, Cass," Cole says, standing to walk toward us. "I need some loving from my son. It's been too long," he says, reaching out for Riley.

"There's Daddy," she whispers, handing over the sleeping baby.

Once he's out of her arms, I adjust us so she's snuggled up against my chest. I'm mindful to keep her on my left side, as the ring is in the right. Thankfully, these jeans are not tight, and I can pass it off as my phone if she notices. I need to keep her busy. Better yet, reaching for a pillow, I set it on my lap.

"My heart is yours," I whisper into her ear. "I can't wait to live this life with you." I don't have to elaborate; she knows what I'm talking about. Since our trip, I've been blunt about what I want, her, a family of our own, and after this conversation, it looks like I'm getting it all. "You're like a genie," I whisper just for her, kissing below her ear.

She looks up at me, a confused expression on her face. "A genie?"

"You grant wishes. I wished for you, and you granted that wish. I wished for you to be my wife, again you granted it. I wished to make babies with you and you also granted that one."

She smiles softly, and I kiss her. I don't care who's watching. Pulling back, she distracts me with pizza and a beer. We spend the next hour or so eating and talking with our friends. I'm the first to stand and call it a night. The guys smirk and the girls swoon when I tell them I need to get my girl home so we can celebrate. I'm sure as soon as the door closes behind us, the guys will fill them in.

I keep both hands on the wheel, afraid she'll notice how clammy they are. I can't wait to ask her to be mine, this time with the ring, the symbol of my love for her, the symbol of the life we're building. I press a little harder on the accelerator.

CHAPTER 30

Cassidy

GAVIN HOLDS ON TO THE wheel like his life depends on it. Usually, he has his hand on my thigh, our fingers laced together, or even my hand on his thigh, with his covering mine. He's always touching me, but not this time. Normally, I would be worried, but every time he glances over at me, there's a smile on his face. A smile that is so full of love and promises of what's yet to come.

When we pull up in front of his house, he turns off the ignition, grabs his keys, and climbs out. I barely have a chance to get the door open before he's gripping my hips and pulling me out. As soon as my feet hit the ground, his hands are cradling my face, and his lips descend on mine. He makes love to my mouth, slow, languid strokes of his tongue against mine. As far as I'm concerned, we can stay out here all night. His kisses are intoxicating.

He pulls back, his eyes locking on mine. His chest is rapidly rising and falling as is my own. His gaze says so much more than words ever could. Love. Lust. Longing.

"Let's get you inside," he finally says.

With my hand locked tightly in his, we make our way inside. Gavin doesn't bother turning on the lights; instead, he leads me through the house and up the stairs in the dark. When we reach his room, he guides me to the bed. "Sit, baby," he whispers.

Under his spell, I do as he asks. When the lamp on the nightstand comes on, I blink at the light, adjusting my eyes. "You take my fucking breath away," he says, tucking a curl behind my ear. "I can't believe I'm the lucky bastard who gets to grow old with you."

Goo. I'm a puddle of mushy gooey lovey mess, and it's all because of the man standing in front of me. He's this badass rock star, covered in ink and ripped in muscles. He's cocky and insistent, and he's all mine. "I could say the same about you," I finally say.

He smiles, then drops to his knees. "I have something for you," he says softly. "Two somethings, actually." He reaches into his pocket and pulls out his phone. I'm not sure what he's doing, but I wait patiently. "Watch this," he says, turning his phone toward me and hits play.

My mom, she's on the screen lying in her hospital bed. She's talking to Gavin, and I know immediately this is the day she was her, not the shell of the woman the disease has made her. Tears sting my eyes, and I look away from the screen to Gavin. "I missed it." I laugh. "I was so caught up in seeing her, can you start it over? I was... I was lost in my head, and I missed what you all were talking about."

His hand behind my neck, he pulls me to him and kisses me softly. "I love you," he says, releasing me and hitting play again.

I keep my eyes on the screen and listen to their conversation. My tears fall unchecked down my cheeks and I don't bother wiping them away. I know there will just be more. When the video ends, I reach for him and wrap my arms as tightly as I can around his neck. "G-Gavin," I cry. "Ho-how did you do this? I mean, I know how, but...." My emotions get the best of me. His arms are around my waist, and he simply holds me as I squeeze the life out of his neck. After a few minutes, I have a little more composure and release my hold on him. Instead, I place my hands on his cheeks and stare into his eyes. "Thank you. You've given me the best gift imaginable. I don't know how to tell you what this means to me. My heart—" I reach for his hands and place his hands over my heart. "—it's racing, to see her like that again and to know..." I choke up. He stays silent, giving me time. "To know that she knows you love me, that we're going to be married. God, Gavin. This... it's everything. I love you. You are everything that is good in my life. You've brought me back to life and this, it's unexpected, and I will cherish it, cherish you always." Those blue eyes of his are shining brightly with love and happiness. I can't look away as I commit this moment to memory.

"I can't remember the exact moment you stole my heart. I don't know that it was one single moment, but lots of little moments. Anytime I spent with you, only made the yearning I felt more pronounced. Then one day, I realized that no one else mattered. It's just you. You were all I could see, all I wanted. When Zach was born, I knew I wanted that with you." He pauses, and his hands fall from my thighs to his sides. The next thing I know he's holding up a little black velvet box. When he opens it, I gasp. The most gorgeous ring I've ever seen before in my life is nestled inside. "I promise to love you, to honor you, to cherish you all the days of my life. Cass, baby, will you marry me?"

I nod, tears clouding my eyes. "Yes. A hundred times over, yes," I say, launching myself at him. He falls back onto the floor, and I land on top of him. His hands cup my face and he wipes my tears with his thumbs.

"I didn't get to give you your ring." He laughs.

Sitting up, I straddle his hips. Still on his back, he removes the ring from its case and slides it on my finger, placing a feather-soft kiss over it. I hold my hand out and admire it. "It's beautiful," I say, my voice barely audible.

"A beautiful ring, for my beautiful girl," he murmurs.

"I don't want to wait," I blurt.

He sits up with me and wraps his arms around my waist. "Tell me what you want, Cass, and I'll make it happen." He kisses my neck. "Gotta say, baby, hearing you say that makes me so damn happy. I want to be married to you yesterday." He nips at my ear.

"The girls and I talked about it today. They said they would help, but really, I just want something… small. Intimate. I'd like for my mom to be there, but taking her out really isn't an option right now. She needs constant supervision, and taking her out of her element upsets her."

"Then we go to her."

"Get married there? In the assisted-living home? Rock star Gavin McIntosh ties the knot at Better Living Assisted Living." I change my voice like one of those reporters on the gossip channels.

"It's our wedding, Cass. We can do whatever the fuck we want. You want your mom there, we can't take her out, so we take the wedding to her."

"You'd do that?" I pause before he can answer. I'd do it for him. "Of course, you would. You're an amazing man, Gavin."

"I'll call them tomorrow and get the ball rolling. When?" he asks, kissing my chin.

"As soon as possible. Just Mom, and our friends, your family. Oh, God, what must your parents think?" I ask worriedly.

"They're going to think I'm a lucky man. They're off traveling the world enjoying life, but I'll call them, and they'll be here. Once we have a date, I'll make it happen."

"We're getting married," I screech and hug him tightly.

"And making babies," he says huskily.

"Babies as in more than one?" I laugh.

"More than one," he confirms, rolling over and switching our positions. He settles between my legs, rocking his hips.

"We're not the only ones," I tell him. He raises his eyebrow in question. "Kacen and Logan." I smile up at him. "Baby Warren number two is on the way,"

"Really?" His eyes light up. "Good for them. But, baby, that means we have a lot of catching up to do."

"You better get started," I say, wrapping my legs around his hips.

"Let's get you out of these clothes." He stands and strips quickly and efficiently, then offers me a hand up. I start to remove my clothes when he tells me he'll be right back. I finish stripping and hear him behind me. Turning, I see he has my purse in his hands. "Your pills, I need them," he says, handing me my purse.

I reach inside, grab the packet, and hand them to him.

He grins, then goes to the bathroom. I wait and then I hear the toilet flush. "You have any more of these?" he asks from the doorway.

"No. I get them filled a month at a time."

"They're gone." His grin lights up his face.

"Yeah?"

"Yep." He pops the *P* and struts back to me.

"You ready for what that means?" I ask him.

"Fuck yes, I am." With that, he picks me up and tosses me on the bed and proceeds to show me just how ready he is, all night long.

CHAPTER 31

GAVIN

WHEN I CALLED BETTER LIVING and told them what we wanted to do, they were hesitant. Then I told them it would be sixteen people, that's including the kids and the minister, and promised to make minimal disturbance to the residents. When I offered a sizeable donation for their trouble, they caved. It was a small price to pay to give Cass what she wants.

That was two weeks ago, and as of today, we have a date. We had to work around their activities they have planned for the residents. We're using the back garden, which is tranquil, and Cass loves it there. We spend a lot of time there when we go to visit her mom. I made sure to tell her that all the residents were invited. My hope is that Margaret will feel more comfortable being there with the others. It won't single her out.

One week from today, I'll be a married man. It doesn't give us much time to plan, but Cass assures me that having her mom there is all she wants. As for me, I would marry her today if she would let me. I'm more than ready to make her Mrs. Gavin McIntosh.

"I'm heading out," she says from her spot behind the couch.

"You sure you don't want me to go with you?"

INSISTENT

"No, you can't see my dress before the wedding."

Reaching into my pocket, I pull out my Am Ex. "I don't care what it costs, you get the dress of your dreams and make sure they have it ready by next Saturday," I tell her.

"I don't have a dream dress," she reminds me. "I just want something simple, no frills. I just want to be yours."

Her words turn me inside out. "I'm wearing jeans and a button-down, right? You sure you don't want me in a tux?" I ask her again.

"Positive. Dark jeans and your black button down are perfect."

"Anything you want," I remind her as she slides into her flip-flops.

Her eyes soften. "Love you. I'll be home later."

"Hey, pick up some stuff for the house while you're out," I yell after her.

She laughs and then I hear the click of the door. She's meeting Stacy, Lauren, and Logan at Logan's to go dress shopping and whatever else shopping she needs for the wedding. I'm sitting in the living room of our new house; we've lived here a week but already with her here with me, it feels like home. We have nothing on the walls, and scarce furnishings, but we'll get there. We bought a bedroom suite and a living room suite, and a few more pieces are to be delivered next week. Everything is coming together.

When my cell rings, I see Kacen's name flash across the screen. "Hey, Kace," I greet him.

"What are you getting into while the girls are gone?" he asks.

"A whole lot of nothing."

"I need to run down to the dealership and drop off my truck for maintenance. You mind picking me up and taking me home?"

I stand and grab my keys from the entryway table. "I'm leaving now. You got my man Drew with you?" I ask him.

"Yeah, we'll have to switch his seat over."

"I'm on my way." When I get to the dealership, I take Drew from Kace while he talks to the guys about whatever it is he's getting done. "Hey there, little man," I say, holding my fist up for him to bump. He doesn't disappoint and then proceeds to give me a sloppy kiss right on the lips.

"You can thank his mother for that," Kacen says with a laugh. "Let me get his seat."

"Did Mommy teach you that?" I ask him.

He nods. "Suga," he says proudly.

I throw my head back in laughter, and the little guy does the same, mimicking me. "You ready for some more cousins to play with?" I ask him.

"We play?" he asks.

"You know it," I tell him, knowing he doesn't really understand what I'm talking about. He heard the word *play* and his concentration is solely on that. We wait while Kacen gets the seat strapped into the back seat of my truck.

"Dada." Drew reaches for his dad and Kacen grins.

"We're having another one," he says with pride in his voice.

"I heard. Congrats, man. I hope to not be too far behind you." He straps his son into his seat, and we head back to his place.

When we get there, I take Drew out back and push him on the swing. I promised him we would play and, with Cass out with the girls, I've got time on my hands. Besides all I have to do is drive across the street to be home. I can't describe how much I love that. I finally feel like I'm home.

"So, a week?"

"Too damn long if you ask me," I reply.

"Now you're starting to sound like Cole."

I laugh. "All you fu—future husbands felt the same way," I say, correcting myself. I almost dropped the f-bomb in front of Drew. Logan would have my ass. If the little guy has a potty mouth, they are not going to be blaming it on Uncle Gavin.

"True." He chuckles.

"Did you think we'd ever get here, man? To the wife and kids, and homes, not just houses but real homes."

"I hoped," he replies. "Although, I wasn't sure about the three of you. I wasn't sure any of you would settle down."

"Just takes the right woman." I grin.

"No truer words have ever been spoken."

We spend the next hour pushing Drew on the swing and playing tag, chasing him around the yard. When he starts to get cranky, Kacen deems it's time for a nap. I give my little buddy a hug and drive across the street to my house. Correction, to the home that Cass and I are building together. I sit in the driveway and think about how fast it all came together. I've wanted her from afar for longer than I can remember and suddenly every wish I've had for us has come true.

I busy myself shopping for a pool table for the basement until Cass comes in with a huge smile on her face. "Hey, baby." I stand to greet her. "Did you find a dress?" I ask.

"A dress, shoes, jewelry. We stopped at the local florist and picked out my bouquet. I even had them make small arrangements for the residents of Better Living. I know it's extravagant, but I thought they would enjoy it."

"I like that idea." I kiss her soft lips. "It's not extravagant. I want this day to be everything you want it to be. It was a sweet thing to do. This way your mom will not feel like she's singled out. My fiancée is so smart," I say, kissing her again.

"You only have one more week to call me that."

"I know. I need to get my fill, but I'll gladly trade it for wife."

"Oh, Lauren invited us over for dinner. We're cooking out. I told her I would bring pasta salad, so I better get busy." She drops a kiss to my lips, and I watch her as she saunters off to the kitchen. I would definitely call this living my best life.

CHAPTER 32

I N THE GARDEN OF THE Better Living Assisted Living Home, Gavin has my hands in his as we face each other. I thought I would be nervous, but when I woke this morning in his arms, because neither one of us wanted to spend the night away from each other, a calm washed over me. I snuck out of bed to the bathroom and watched the video Gavin recorded of my mother. He sent it to me that night, and I've watched it several times.

We had breakfast together and then I left for Lauren's. All the women met there to get ready. They helped with my hair and makeup, and then the dress. It's white satin with spaghetti straps that looks as though it was made to fit my curves. It's long and drags the ground, but once I add my heels, it's perfect. I couldn't wait for Gavin to see me in it. And his face when I walked down the aisle is one I'll never forget.

Now here we are about to say "I do."

"Gavin, repeat after me," the minister says. He proceeds to do as he's instructed, sliding the diamond eternity band on my finger, giving my hands a gentle squeeze. The smile on his face mirrors my own.

"Cassidy, repeat after me." I, too, follow the traditional vows. I wanted something simple, quick, and easy, and that's exactly what we're doing. When I slide his black Tungsten ring on his finger, he mouths, "I love you," as he pulls me a little closer. He knows what comes next and he's ready for it.

"By the power vested in me by the state of Tennessee, I now pronounce you husband and wife. You may kiss your bride."

The words are barely out of the minister's mouth before Gavin has his arms wrapped around me, is lifting me off my feet and crashing his lips into mine. There are whoops and hollers and cheers of congratulations. Almost all of the residents showed up, even my mom. I stopped to see her before the ceremony, and she didn't know me. But she did, however, congratulate me on my nuptials and thanked me for inviting her. I watched the video one more time before I walked down the aisle.

"I love you, Mrs. McIntosh," he says against my lips.

"I love you too, husband."

"Fuck yes," he whispers. "Say it again, baby."

"Husband," I repeat, knowing that's the only part he wants.

Our friends come up and congratulate us and head toward the tent we have set up with a DJ and finger foods. It's a small affair, and I could not have asked for more. Once we've said hello and received congratulations from all our guests, we head toward the tent. Just inside sits my mother in her wheelchair. I stop in front of her, and a tear slides down her cheek.

"Cassidy," she whispers.

It's a good thing Gavin has a firm grip on my waist, or I might have fallen to my knees at the sound of her voice. "Hey, Mom," I say, not bothering to fight the tears. Everything else fades away. All I can see and all I can hear is her. "I missed you," I tell her honestly.

"You're married." She smiles. "I didn't know, until the end. It reminded me so much of me and your father."

Kneeling, I take her hand. "I'm glad you're here," I tell her. I don't know how long she'll be lucid. "Gavin is a great man. I love him very much." I feel his silent strength behind me as he rests his hands on my bare shoulders, giving me this moment with her.

"Handsome too," she muses.

I laugh through my tears. "Very handsome. I love you, Mom," I say, leaning in to kiss her cheek.

"Oh, my sweet girl. I love you, too. Be happy, Cassidy." She looks over my shoulder. "Young man, I expect you'll take good care of my baby and future grandchildren?"

"Yes, ma'am," he agrees. "Cassidy is my heart, Margaret."

She nods. "Go on, go visit with all your friends who came to see you."

"No. We're good right here," Gavin insists. "There's nothing more important than this moment right here."

"Tell me about you. Where will you live?" she asks.

I go on to tell her about the house and how we're living on the same street as Gavin's bandmates, who are more like brothers. I wave all of them over and introduce them to her. The girls have tears in their eyes, and if I'm not mistaken, the guys' eyes are glassy, too. There is no beer because Stacy and Lauren are breastfeeding, Logan is pregnant, and I hope to be one day soon. So, it has to be this moment.

"Let's move you ladies to a table," Gavin says. He steps behind Mom's wheelchair and guides her to the nearest table. I take the seat next to her, and Gavin the one next to me.

"There is so much I want to know. Do you plan on having kids? How is your job? Oh my, the list goes on and on," she says.

"We want kids," I say. "Our home, it's got six bedrooms."

"You plan on filling all those rooms?" she asks.

"As many as she'll let me," Gavin chimes in. "We can add on if we need to."

Mom chuckles. "He's a keeper. I always wanted more children, but it just wasn't in the cards for us. You are the light of my life, Cassidy."

"I love you, Mom." I say it again because she's lucid and she's with me and this is my wedding day. I can't seem to say it enough.

"Work is good. I was worried at first since Gavin is my boss, but it all worked out in the end."

"That's great, dear. What did you say your name was again?" she asks.

My heart plummets, and I can't fight the burn of the hot tears behind my eyes.

"Cass, baby, I've got you," Gavin assures me. "I've got you," he says again, wrapping an arm around my shoulders.

"Margaret," one of the nurses comes rushing over. "Would you like some cake?" she asks her.

"Oh, yes. Congratulations," she says to us as the nurse pulls her chair from the table and wheels her away.

I turn into Gavin's chest and let the tears fall. He doesn't tell me it's going to be okay. He just holds me, letting me work it all out of my system. "I'm glad she was here, you know. That she got to see us, and that she recognized us. It was more than I could have asked for. I just wish... Gah! I hate this disease."

"I know, baby," Gavin soothes. "I hate it, too, but she got to see you happy. She got to see you in your dress, and she knows that one day soon she's going to be a grandmother. We have to hope that somewhere down the line she'll remember it all."

Before I can reply, I feel three sets of arms wrap around us. Stacy, Logan, and Lauren are hugging us.

"We know this is hard, but there are things to celebrate today. Your mom got to see you in your dress and meet your husband," Lauren says.

"And you two have a wedding dance to take care of," Stacy says.

"Yeah, how else are we going to get our husbands out on that dance floor? We're waiting for the two of you," Logan informs us.

"What do you say, wife? You want to dance with your husband?"

"Yes."

"I told you I love that word when it falls from these soft lips." He traces his thumb across my bottom lip.

"Come on, lovebirds," Stacy jokes, tugging on each of our hands to get us up and on the dance floor.

We spend the next couple of hours laughing, dancing, and eating cake. Gavin even led my mom out on the dance floor. Cole, Kacen, and Tristan did the same with a few of the other female residents so she wouldn't feel singled out. It was the perfect day, and I could not have wished for more on my wedding day. I have my husband to thank for that.

CHAPTER 33

I'T'S NOT EVEN DAYLIGHT OUTSIDE and I'm wide awake. My wife and I got in late last night from our honeymoon in Fiji. It was a week filled with making love to my wife and lounging on the beach, one I am sure to never forget, and neither of us were ready to come back home. But today we head back to work. My wife insisted, stating she'd taken too much time off recently. I had to get the guys to threaten to fire her for us to take our honeymoon. It's going to take her a while to get used to the fact that she's not just an employee now. She's mine. All fucking mine.

I'm on my side, head propped up on my elbow just watching her sleep as memories of her naked in the crystal-clear water runs through my mind. We stayed at a private beach, and we took full advantage. Sliding my hand under the sheet, I rest my hand on her belly. I can't help but wonder if my son or daughter is growing there. Cass warned me that it could take a while, that she's been on birth control for a long time and sometimes these things take time. I get that, I do. However, I have this feeling, deep in my gut, the same one that told me I couldn't live without her, that tells me we're going to be holding our baby very soon.

Her eyes flutter open and a slow smile spreads across her face. "Morning."

INSISTENT

"Morning, my beautiful wife." I lean in and kiss her lips.

"What time is it?" she asks, yawning.

"Just after six."

"Why are you up so early?" Her brow furrows in concern.

"I like watching you sleep," I say, soothing her brow with my thumb.

"Creeper," she says with a laugh.

"What, can a husband not watch his wife?"

"It's been over a week, Gav, how many times are you going to keep saying that?"

"For the rest of my life. It's an honor to call you my wife."

"Smooth talker." She smiles. "Since we're up, we might as well make some breakfast."

"You sleep. I'll do it." I move to climb out of bed.

"I'll help. No way am I falling back asleep now that I'm up."

"You can set your sexy ass on the chair and watch. I'm making you breakfast. Bacon and eggs okay?" I ask.

"Who knew husbands could be so bossy?" she asks. "Yes, that sounds perfect."

"Not bossy, insistent, remember?" I wink. She's told me repeatedly that I'm too insistent, but I can't help that I know what I want, and it all revolves around her.

I grab some shorts from our dresser and a T-shirt for Cass. We make our way downstairs and, just as I instructed, she sits on the island in the kitchen and watches me make us breakfast.

"I forgot to tell you. I was texting with Stacy yesterday and told her that we would keep Riley for a few hours tonight so that she and Cole could go out to dinner."

"Good. We're going to need some practice," I tell her.

"Gav, you know it could take months even years for me to get pregnant. Some people try and it never happens for them," she says softly.

"If that happens, there are plenty of babies out there who need loving parents, and a safe home to call their own, and we have one big enough to offer it to them. However, I can feel it, Cass." I set our plates on the island and slide my hand under my shirt she's wearing to rest it on her

176

bare stomach. "I think it's already happened."

"Oh, Gavin. I'm so afraid you're going to be disappointed."

"Never," I say firmly. "Do I want to see you growing with our child? Yes, I do. Do I want to know that I'm the reason for the changes in your body and be there when you bring this tiny human that we created into the world? Hell yes. But, if that's not how it works for us, I still get to see you be an amazing mother. I still get to be a daddy and that's what's important."

"I love you, Gavin McIntosh."

"I love you, too, wife." I grin. "Now eat up. Work is calling."

When we get to the office, Cass goes to her office while I go to the one that I share with the guys. It was hard for me to keep my distance before, always thinking of reasons to stop in and see her, ask her questions. Now that she's my wife, it's even harder. I just want to be next to her all the damn time.

"When does this… fade out?" I ask Kacen, who is the only other person here right now.

"When does what fade out?"

"The need to be next to her. It's fucking with me that she's just down the hall and I'm in here. There's something wrong with me, right? Some kind of weird attachment thing?" I ask him.

He throws his head back and laughs. "Well, if there is, then I have it, too. Fuck, man, we all do. You see how we all are."

"You and Logan have been married the longest. You still feel this… need to be beside her all the time?"

"Every hour of the day," he confirms.

"Well, at least I know I'm not losing my mind," I say, running my fingers through my hair. "She'll rip my ass if I bother her, though. I know she's trying to get caught up from being off and she hated missing last week."

"Get used to it, man. They love us, but we've all picked some pretty independent ladies to walk through life with us. And just a warning, they will band together. The four of them will gang up on you. Trust me, I've been there. Even before Cassidy was your wife, she was close to mine. I've been on the receiving end of that. Just agree and all is good."

"I can't say no to her, but thanks for the warning."

INSISTENT

"Gavin," Cass says from the doorway. "Would you mind telling me why the GMC dealer just called to tell me they're running earlier than expected for my delivery?" she asks, hands on her hips.

"Shit," I mumble. "They were supposed to call me," I tell her.

"What exactly are they delivering?"

"Well, your car is great, but you're going to need something safer and bigger." I glance down at her still flat stomach. "Hopefully soon, so I bought you a new car."

"Gavin!" she scolds me. "Really? Don't you think we should have talked about this?" she huffs.

Kacen is sitting at his desk grinning like a fool. Asshole. "Baby, it needed to happen. Your car is older, and even if we're not pregnant right away, it's safer for you." I try to reason with her.

"Okay, but we should talk about these kinds of things. What if I hate it?"

"It's a new Yukon Denali, fully loaded, you're going to love it."

Her eyes light up and she tries to hide her smile. "Fine. But next time we talk about this, and what are we going to do with my car?"

"We're donating it." I know this is something she will be happy about. "Someone who is struggling will get it. It will be a great vehicle for them to get back on their feet."

"You're forgiven," she says, then turns and walks away.

"Good touch with the donating the car thing. She let you off easy."

"I was expecting more than that, too." I grin. "We've got this married thing down," I say, holding my fist out for him. He pushes his into mine as we laugh.

I'm sure there will be many more disagreements, but there is no one on earth I'd rather argue with more. Not to mention tonight when we get home, we're going to need make-up sex. Hell, I love married life.

CHAPTER 34

 Cassidy

Today is our one-month wedding anniversary, and I'm officially five days late. I've kept it to myself, and even though I'm pretty regular, there's still a chance that I'm just late. There have been a lot of life changes in the last two months, which could be the reason. I could also be pregnant. I've not mentioned it to Gavin. I've been waiting to see if Aunt Flow decides to visit, and she's yet to arrive. It's been five long days.

In bed, Gavin's head is resting on my chest as he sleeps peacefully. I decided that once I hit the five-day mark, I would tell him. I even slipped out to pick up lunch Friday and bought a few tests. You can't take just one. Gavin and the guys were busy with Shattered Heart, working on writing some new material for their debut album. I'm trying not to get my hopes up, but it's hard. Gavin might be the one who's always talking about us getting pregnant, but I've always wanted to be a mom. Mine was the perfect role model, and I want the chance to be just like her. I want to be a mother. I'm afraid to be disappointed, but I know these things take time, just like I keep telling him. However, here we are one month later and I'm late. He said he had a gut feeling. Could he have been right?

My plan was to let him sleep, but I have to pee and everything I've read online said that first thing in the morning is the best time to take the test for earlier detection. So I have to wake my slumbering husband and tell him what I'm doing before I pee down my leg. That's what I get for keeping things from him.

"Gav." I run my fingers through his hair, and he moans softly. "Babe, I need to pee," I tell him. If he doesn't wake up, I can take the tests and let them sit, then wake him up. "Gavin," I say again, this time shaking his shoulder.

"What's wrong?" he asks, raising his head to look at me.

"I have to pee," I tell him.

"Sorry, come back to bed," he mumbles.

I climb out of bed and rush to the bathroom. I barely get the first box of tests open, which contains two, before I pee down my leg. It's awkward as hell, and I'm glad he's still sleeping. I can only imagine his insistent self would want to be in here and that would make it even more awkward. Sure, he's my husband, and he's seen all of me, but this is... uncomfortable even for me.

Capping both tests, I set them on the counter, then wash my hands. I refuse to look at them and am determined I'll do it with Gavin. I don't bother putting the other tests away, not yet. Instead, I make my way back to bed. Gavin is awake, his eyes hooded as he holds the blanket up for me. I slide underneath and snuggle up next to him.

"I have something to tell you," I tell him.

"What is it, baby?" he asks softly.

"I'm late."

"Late for what, Cass. It's Sunday."

"My period, I'm late."

He sits up, causing me to fall back on the bed. "How late is late?" he asks, his eyes now bright and alert.

"Five days."

"Five? Why are you just now telling me?" He jumps out of bed and rushes to the dresser, pulling out some sweats and sliding them over his slim hips.

"What are you doing?"

"Going to get us some pregnancy tests. I knew I should have bought some just to have," he mumbles to himself.

"Gavin." I try to get his attention, but he rushes toward the bathroom, I assume to brush his teeth. Instead of trying again, I grab his T-shirt off the floor, slip it over my head, and follow him. I'm leaning against the bathroom door watching as he brushes his teeth. He has yet to notice the tests, but he will when he reaches for the towel. At least I think he will.

He shuts off the water, drops his toothbrush to the counter, and reaches for the towel. He freezes and I know he's seen them.

"Cassidy!" he yells for me.

"I tried to tell you," I say, trying to fight my laughter.

"Have you seen these?" he asks.

"Nope. I took them and then left them on the counter to come and talk to you. You were out of bed before I could tell you I bought tests already."

He picks them up, then turns to face me. His face is void of emotion, and my heart sinks. That must mean they're negative. "So you don't know what they say?" he asks slowly. It's like he's preparing me for disappointment.

"No. What do they say?" I ask. I brace my hands on the doorframe for support.

He looks down at the two tests in his hands. "They say…" He looks up and smiles softly. "That we're having a baby." His smile grows wide. "Cass, a baby, we're having a baby." He rushes toward me. He has his arms around me and is swinging me around before I can process what he said.

"Gavin, stop." I laugh. He stops spinning but keeps his hold on me. "They're positive?" I ask, needing to hear it again.

"They are, both of them. How many did you buy? You want to take a few more? I can go get them, but these say *Pregnant,* Cass."

"It could be a bad batch, you know. False positives. Maybe I should take the others."

"Whatever you want, baby. I'll go grab a couple bottles of water. You get the tests out and ready." He sets me back on my feet, kisses me hard and fast, and rushes out of the room. I hear his feet thunder down the stairs. I look for the tests to see for myself and realize he must still have them with him.

He's back in no time and opens a bottle of water, handing it to me.

INSISTENT

"Can I see those?" I point to the tests.

"Drink," he says, pointing to the bottle in my hands as he passes me the tests in the other.

He reaches for the box of the two tests I took and starts reading it. "Cass, this says that these are 99 percent accurate up to as early as five days late. We're pregnant, baby." He grins.

"Let's take these, and if we get the same result, we'll call and make an appointment."

I down both bottles of water in about twenty minutes. About ten minutes after that, I have to pee again. I'm able to convince him, surprisingly, to let me pee on the sticks alone. I have a feeling if he were not still gripping the first two positive tests, I wouldn't have gotten off that easily. Capping the tests and setting them on the counter, I wash my hands. Gavin hears the water turn on and comes into the room. "Five minutes," he says.

"Might as well be five hours," I say, knowing this will be the longest five minutes of my life.

"I can help with that." He pushes me up against the bathroom wall. "We're having a baby," he whispers against my lips. He kisses me, his tongue lazily stroking against mine. His hands are cupping my face, and just like every other time, I get lost in him. The feel of his hard body pressing me against the wall, the softness of his lips, and his calloused hands that hold my face. When he pulls back, he rests his forehead against mine. "I love you, Cass, so fucking much. I love you," he murmurs.

"You're going to have to clean up that potty mouth of yours," I tease.

"Done. We can get a swear jar. Our kid will be the richest around." He laughs.

"Yeah, and the kid on the playground the other parents warn their kids about."

He throws his head back and laughs. "It's been more than five minutes," he says once his laughter is under control.

"You look."

He grins and releases me to reach for the tests. "Hell fucking yes," he says excitedly. "Baby McIntosh." He grins, handing me two more positive tests.

Tears prick my eyes. *We're having a baby.* I'm going to be a mom. I wish mine were here so I could tell her. Maybe, maybe she'll have another good day so I can tell her. If not, I know she's with me, just like she said. She's always with me. I'll make sure my son or daughter knows how amazing she is. They'll know her just as I did growing up. The her before the disease took over her life.

Gavin kisses my neck. "We need to celebrate."

I look up at my husband and nod. I need to be close to him… the man I love, the father of my unborn child. He leads me back to bed and pulls his shirt over my head. Dropping to his knees, he kisses my flat belly. "I'm your daddy," he murmurs. "I love you so much already."

Tears fall unchecked as he guides me on the bed and proceeds to make love to me.

CHAPTER 35

GAVIN

MY WIFE IS TWENTY WEEKS pregnant today and so fucking beautiful she takes my breath away. Her belly looks like she has a basketball under her shirt and I can't keep my hands off her. I talk to her stomach all the time, letting my baby know how much I love them already. And my wife, it's more than her belly I can't keep my hands off. She's sexy as fuck, and it might make me a pervert, but when I look at her and see her body changing with a piece of me and her, something we created out of love, I get hard just thinking about it.

"Gav, you ready?" she calls up the stairs.

We found out yesterday what we're having, but we've kept it to ourselves until today. We went to visit her mom, but she didn't recognize us. We still told her about our baby, and even though I know it hurts her, Cass handled it well. Today, we're headed over to Tristan and Lauren's for Zach's first birthday. It's hard to believe it's been a year since he was born. So much has changed. We plan on telling everyone what we're having since we'll all be together.

"The gift's on the front porch," Cass says when I hit the bottom of the steps.

"You should have let me get it," I scold her.

"Come on, Gavin. I'm pregnant, not disabled. I can carry a gift bag with a toy drum set and a fire truck." She laughs.

"But you don't have to with me around."

"Come on, you." She grins and pulls the door open.

I'm quick to grab the bag in one hand and her hand with the other. We walk down the street to Tristan's place. "Get over here," Logan says when she spots us. We make our way to the back patio. I set the gift on the small table with other packages and then pull a chair out for Cass. "You have to tell us," Logan demands.

"Tell you what?" I play dumb.

"Gavin!" She smacks my arm.

I turn to Cass. "You want to tell them?"

"Go ahead," she says, laughing. She knows it's been killing me as much as it's been killing Logan to find out.

"It's a girl."

"Yes!" Logan cheers. "Our daughters will be so close," she gushes, rubbing her very pregnant belly. She's due in a few weeks with baby number two.

All the women pass out hugs, and the guys do as well. I'm still grinning, but I think that's been my look since the day Cass said we could try to be an us. Now here we are married, with a sweet baby girl on the way.

"Well," Tristan says, "since we're making announcements," he turns to look at Lauren, and she nods, "baby Lewis number two is baking." He pats Lauren's still flat belly. Another round of cheers and congratulations are passed around with more hugs.

"Well, damn." Cole looks at Stacy. She just smiles and nods. Cole beams at her, then kisses her softly before looking at all of us. "The Hamptons will be adding to their count as well," he tells us.

Riley is under a year, around eight or so months, I guess. I'm not surprised though. Cole has always been vocal about wanting more kids. We all have, now that we've found the loves of our lives.

Hours later, I'm sitting on the deck listening to our wives talk about pregnancy and baby showers. Cass's laughter reaches me, and I smile because of it. Today has been great. My boy Zach made out on gifts, and Tristan was stoked about the drums. Apparently, he tried to buy them, but Lauren shut him down, saying it's a lot of noise until he is older and can learn how to play. I just shrugged unapologetically. I'm sure she'll pay me back once our baby girl is born. I'm good with it. I have a strong suspicion that, just as it is with her mother, I'll never be able to tell her no. I'm glad that Drew, Riley, and Zach are older than her. She's going to need older brothers to protect her.

"What's got you so lost in thought?" Cole asks.

"Just that I'm glad there are boys in the family to be the older brothers to my daughter."

"Or to steal her heart," Logan yells over.

"Woman!" I laugh.

"It could happen," Kacen says.

"Yeah, I guess it could happen for your little girl, too." I see it in his face; he didn't think that far ahead, then again neither did I until his wife chimed in.

He takes a long drink of water. "Sure, when she's thirty," he says, making us all laugh.

"Nah, man. I'd be proud to have any of those boys be with my daughter, when she's older of course," I tell them honestly.

"We were heathens," Kacen reminds me. "Well, you guys were heathens, I was just along for the ride." He chuckles.

"That may be true, but like our fathers before us, we were raised to love our women and take care of them. I have no doubt that your boys will be the exact same way."

"Can we not talk about this?" Tristan says. "If we have a girl, she's not allowed to date. Not ever."

"Hear, hear," Cole chimes in.

I can hear our wives laughing at us, but none of us care. Our topic switches to work, not because we're overwhelmed and need to hash it out, but because music is in our blood.

Hours later, we're lying in bed. Cass is sound asleep and my hand is on our daughter. Soon it will be us, our little family that's hosting birthday parties. This woman lying in my arms has brought so much to my life. I thank God every single day for creating the perfect woman for me. That's my last thought before drifting off to sleep.

CHAPTER 36

I brace myself, grabbing the sheets as another contraction hits. "That's a big one," Gavin says, staring at the monitor that tracks my contractions. I love my husband, but I'm ready to strangle him.

"Gavin," I grit out.

"What, baby?" he asks sweetly.

"I can feel how big they are. I don't need a fucking reminder," I tell him, for what feels like the one-hundredth time since I've been here. My water broke about 1:00 a.m. and it's now ten at night. Nineteen hours of labor and a husband who reminds me I'm having a contraction. I can feel that shit, trust me.

"Sorry, Cass. Here, have some more ice chips." He holds a cup and spoonful of ice to my lips.

"I don't want more ice chips." My voice is a little harsher than what I intended but another contraction hits.

"Here co—" I squeeze the hell out of his hand which shuts him up.

"I think it's time, Gav. I feel a lot of pressure," I tell him.

"Let me call for the nurse." He reaches behind my bed and pushes the call button.

INSISTENT

The nurse strolls into the room and lifts my blanket to check on me. "Oh my, yes, I can see the head," she says. "Hold strong, Cassidy. I'll just get the doctor." She jogs out of the room and yells down the hall, to I'm guessing another nurse to page the doctor.

"I want to see," Gavin says, pulling the blanket back and I smack him on the back of the head.

"I need you up here," I say through gritted teeth as another contraction hits. "I need to push," I say, holding onto his hand for dear life.

"Breathe, Cass. You're doing great, baby. You ready to meet, baby girl?" he asks.

"Cassidy," Dr. Brown greets me. "How are you doing?"

"Ready to push," I tell him.

A flurry of activity happens: my legs are placed in stirrups, a light is brought down from the ceiling, and then he's telling me to push. "On three, Cassidy," he says.

On three, I push hard and the pressure is uncomfortable. I'm thanking my lucky stars for epidurals, even if I had to have two.

"You're doing great, Cass." Gavin cheers me on. He's holding one of my legs while the nurse has the other pushed up to my chest.

"She's crowning," the doctor says.

"I have to see this," Gavin says, and this time before I can stop him, he's looking past the blankets. His face pales and he steps back to me. "You're incredible," he whispers, his hot breath next to my ear. "I love you, Cassidy McIntosh. Thank you for giving me the greatest gifts of my life. You and our daughter."

"Cassidy, I need one more big push. Give it all you've got," Dr. Brown says from between my legs.

"Catch her, Doc," Gavin warns him, making the nurse and doctor chuckle.

"I assure you, Mr. McIntosh, your daughter is in good hands. On three, Cassidy, all you've got," he reminds me. "One, two, three," he says, and I bear down, chin to my chest, and push as hard as I can. Gavin and the nurse hold my legs to my chest and just when I'm about to give up, the pressure is gone and I hear her cry.

"Healthy baby girl," the doctor says. Gavin moves down to cut the cord, and they wipe her down and place her on my bare chest.

"Hello, sweet girl," I whisper through my tears.

"Damn good job, Mommy," Gavin whispers. "She's beautiful, Cass. You did it." His voice cracks.

"You want to hold her?" I ask. He swallows hard and nods. The nurse helps transfer our daughter from my arms to his.

"Hey, sweetheart," he coos at her. "I'm your daddy. I'm glad to finally meet you." He stares down at her, a look of pure love and awe on his face.

"All right, Daddy. We need to take her and give her a bath and run some tests."

"Where are you taking her?" he asks, getting defensive.

"We're not leaving the room." She points over to the corner where a station is set up. "We'll be right over there." He nods and reluctantly passes our daughter off to the nurse.

Gavin buries his face in my neck and tells me over and over how much he loves me and our daughter. Hot tears spill onto my neck, and I can't seem to prevent my own from falling. What seems likes mere minutes, but I'm sure is much longer, the same nurse is placing my daughter back in my arms and helping me try to nurse. Our little girl is a champ and latches on without an issue.

"I've never seen anything more beautiful," Gavin says softly, tracing his finger over her forehead.

We block out the activity in the room and focus on our miracle. "She needs a name," he reminds me.

"Yeah, what are you thinking?" We both agreed to have names in mind, but we wanted to see her first. Meet her.

"You go first," he says.

"I like Cora, for a first name."

"Cora," he says, testing it out. "I love it. I thought we could give her your mom's name, too. Margaret as a middle name."

"How about her middle name as Renee? Cora Renee McIntosh," I say, putting it all together. "My mom's middle name is Renee and was also my grandmother's."

"Welcome to the family, Cora Renee," he says, leaning in to place a kiss on her tiny head.

INSISTENT

Once she's finished feeding, I pass her off to Gavin, and he settles into the chair next to my bed and snuggles her close. I watch as he unwraps her and counts all ten fingers and all ten toes. "I love you, Cora." He looks up and his eyes find mine. "Thank you, Cass. For loving me, for being my wife, for this precious little girl. I can't wait until we can do this again."

"Hold up there, Daddy," I say, yawning. "Let me recuperate from this little angel first."

"Mommy needs to sleep," he tells our slumbering daughter. "Rest, baby. We'll be here when you wake up." Reaching out, I place my hand on his shoulder, I just need to feel connected to them. It's not long before my eyes are drifting shut.

CHAPTER 37

GASS LEFT EARLY THIS MORNING to go to the office. Shattered Heart's first album is about to release, and she had a press release or something that she wanted to wrap up and get sent off. I told her I would stay and wait for Cora to wake up and then be in later. Little Miss had a rough night. She's teething and it's hard for her to sleep.

At six months old, she's the light of our lives. I never thought I would say this, but if we as a band Soul Serenade never tour again, it will be fine by me. I can't imagine being away from them for that long. And to raise her on a tour bus… that's not the life I want for her. I know without saying it the guys feel the same way. We've made enough money that our kids will never have to work a day in their lives, hell, their kids even. Now, we get to sit back and coast, raise our kids, fall asleep next to our wives. Nothing is better than that.

I hear a whimper come through the monitor, telling me she's waking. I'm already up and ready for the day; I wasn't going to miss the opportunity to shower with my sexy wife. I came back upstairs to watch TV until Cora work up. Turning off the TV, I head down the hall to her room. She's in her crib, fussing and wanting to be held. I'm also sure she needs a diaper change.

"Hey, sweet girl," I say, reaching for her. Her little arms flap in the air in excitement. Her head full of curls—the same color as her mother's—thick and blonde is sticking up everywhere. She reminds me so much of Cass my heart aches. As soon as I pick her up, she snuggles into my shoulder. "You had a rough night, huh?" I know she can't tell me, but I do it anyway. I talked to her before she was born, no point in stopping now. Cass says it's why she's a daddy's girl, so much so she refused to nurse, but when I offered her a bottle, she took it. She was three months old when that happened. After talking with the pediatrician, we switched her over to formula, and I gotta say, I love being able to feed her.

"Let's get you changed." I make quick work of changing her diaper and dressing her for the day. Cass already packed her diaper bag and said she would leave it downstairs. I told her I would get it, but she insisted. She smarted off something about her "insistence" shouldn't bother me. My wife, she's got jokes.

Once I have a happy fed baby, I load her up in my truck, pink diaper bag and all, and head toward Soul Records. We each hired our own nannies, so to speak, but they only work when we're all at the office. Our wives work with us, all except Lauren, but we changed that, splitting Cass's duties with her. It works for us. We're family owned and operated. On the first level, you would never know that the upstairs is baby/toddler heaven. With it being a studio, the walls are soundproof so the kids can play as loud as they want as they grow older and we never have to worry about disrupting business.

"There's Mommy," I whisper, stopping just in the doorway of Cass's office.

"Hey, you two." She stands and reaches for Cora, who goes willingly into her mom's arms. "You feeling better, sweetie?" she asks her.

"She drank her entire bottle with no complaints. She seems to be better today." I snag an arm around Cass's waist and press a kiss to her lips. Cora leans in and slobbers on my cheek. "Love you," I tell my wife, then turn and kiss Cora's cheek, telling her the same.

I'm not sure what I've done in life to get me to where I am today. I can tell you that my heart is full. I've had a great career, and we're lucky to not have to worry about money. I have my beautiful wife and daughter, and the best friends and family a guy could ask for. I'm looking forward to what the next sixty or so years has in store for us.

"Mommy picked up something for daddy on the way to work today.

You want to give it to him?" Cass asks our daughter.

I chuckle when Cora squeals, sensing her mom's excitement but has no idea why. Cass reaches beside her desk and grabs a small white gift bag. It must be light because she places Cora's hand around it and together they hand me the bag. "Thank you." I kiss Cora on the cheek and snag my arm around my wife, kissing her lips with our daughter bouncing in her arms, surely wanting to get in on the action. "It's not my birthday," I say, pulling away from the kiss.

"Oh, this is a 'just because I love you' gift." She smiles brightly.

The day she decided to stop fighting and that we could be together, I thought I couldn't love her more. I was wrong. Every fucking day she buries herself a little deeper into my heart, winding her arms around my soul. To this day, I still crave her touch, her kisses, the feel of her in my arms. She is, and forever will be, my heart.

"Open it already," she says impatiently, laughter in her voice.

Carefully, I remove the tissue paper, and nestled inside is a little pink piece of fabric. Confused, I find her eyes and they're shining as she nods at me to keep going. Grabbing the fabric from the bag, I unfold it to see a little pink T-shirt. My eyes find my wife's again and she's laughing, her eyes welling with tears.

"Read it," she urges.

Flipping the shirt over, I read the words that are written in white letters. "I'm the big sister" it says. I read it again, and then again just to make sure I'm not seeing things. Then I look at her. My beautiful wife loses the battle with her tears as one slides down her cheek.

"We're pregnant?" I ask her.

She nods, giving me a watery smile. "It's soon." She looks over at Cora in her arms and kisses the top of her head. "But you said you wanted lots of babies."

"I think I said, I wanted lots of babies with you. There is a difference." I grip the shirt tightly in my fist as I step into her yet again. The hand gripping the shirt goes around her waist while the other lands on her flat belly. Cora reaches down to mimic me. "Only babies with you," I whisper, kissing the corner of her mouth. I can feel the lump in the back of my throat from the news.

"I'm sorry. The pill must have failed. There is that chance, although you never think it will be with you." She's rambling, taking my silence as fear. She knows me better than that.

"Baby." I cup her face in the palm of my hand. "I'm glad it failed. Nothing is a greater gift in life than making babies with you. Nothing." I drop a kiss to her forehead, then take Cora, who is reaching for me. I pull Cass into our embrace. "We'll add onto the house if we have to," I tell her, causing her to laugh.

"Let's fill up the rooms we have before we start talking additions to the house." She snuggles into my chest.

"Cole and Stacy still have us beat. We'll have to try sooner next time," I say, only half joking.

"We're going to have two less than a year and a half apart. I think we're good."

"It's the trying that we're good at." My pants grow a little tighter just thinking about it.

"Yeah," she readily agrees. "We are good at that." With one arm around my waist, the other reaches up and rests on Cora's back.

"Thank you for this life," I whisper. "There is no one else in this entire world I'd want this with. It's you and only you. It will only ever be you," I say, holding her close. Cora rests her head on my shoulder, mimicking her mother. "You, too, sweet girl, and your little brother or sister," I tell her. She just sticks her fist in her mouth and chews. She's teething and is a slobber box; my shirt is testament to that. I wouldn't change it for anything. The money, the fame, the success, none of it means anything without my family by my side.

EPILOGUE

Three Years Later

'M SITTING IN THE BACKYARD with my six-week old son, Garrett, sleeping peacefully against my bare chest. Today is just another day, but my wife decided to have a cookout. One call to Logan, Stacy, and Lauren and plans were made. Not that I mind. They're family and having this little corner of our gated community to just us and our kids, it's like living in Mayberry, only on steroids. Our road is a dead end, which means the dads set up their lawn chairs toward the middle of the street and let them run crazy. They know they can't pass where we sit and are not allowed to play in that particular spot unless we are out there with them. Not that we ever get any traffic. But when it's your babies, you can never be too careful.

"He's out," Kacen says from his seat beside me. He has his daughter, Paige, in his arms giving her a bottle. I think she's eight months old, or around there. I lost track after we all had our firsts. Cass is the one that always remembers the birthdays of the family.

"He is. Eat, sleep, shit, repeat at this age." I laugh.

"Yeah, but damn, it's hard to see them grow up. It feels like yesterday we brought her home from the hospital." He motions to Paige who is eating without a care in the world in her dad's arms.

"Hey, y'all need a beer?" Cole walks over to ask us.

I remember the days he would have yelled it out with not a care in the world, but as parents, you learn to be mindful of sleeping babies. Especially Cole. Their second, Colton, had colic and the little guy was miserable for the first few months. Looking out in the yard, I watch as he plays with the other kids—a happy healthy three-year-old. I think he's three. I'll have to remember to ask Cass.

"Yeah," Kacen and I answer at the same time.

"Tristan and Lauren are on their way," he tells us. "Justin had an accident."

"Ah, the joys of potty training." Kacen laughs. "We had a hell of a time with Drew, finally threw some Cheerios in the toilet and we made a game of it. Worked like a charm."

"Did you tell T that?" I laugh.

"Yep, he and Lauren said it worked like a charm with Zach."

Cole comes back with four bottles of beer, setting the extra on the table, I assume for Tristan, who comes walking over as soon as he takes his seat.

"That's for you." Cole points his bottle to the one on the table.

"Thanks. Sorry we're late. J had an accident. He was so excited to come play with his friends, he waited too late to go to the potty," Tristan explains.

"Been there." Cole laughs.

We're quiet for a few minutes as we watch our kids run and play, while our wives work on setting up the food. We were instructed we were on kid duty because they needed girl time, and they would take care of the food. None of us complained; it's not a hardship to watch your children run and play, or in my case, sleep peacefully in your arms while his siblings run and play.

"Stacy's pregnant," Cole says, tipping his beer to his lips. "Number four. You would think that the excitement would simmer a little, but fuck, it's not. And the kids, Riley, Colt, and Sienna are all excited as well. Sienna doesn't really understand yet, but the boys, I think they get it, especially Riley."

We all congratulate him, when Tristan speaks up. "We're trying for number three. We're hoping to give Zach and Justin a little sister this time."

More congratulations, then Kacen speaks up. "I've been trying to convince Logan that we need at least one more. She says that Drew, Shane, and Paige keep us busy enough." He laughs.

"It took me two years to get this little guy after Grant was born." I kiss my Garrett on top of his tiny head. "Although, Cora keeps telling her mom she needs a sister, so maybe I can convince her of another one." I think about my wife, and the love that shines in her eyes when it comes to our kids, and I know without a doubt, that we'll be trying for another little girl. Not right away, but I can see it happening for us. No matter the sex of the baby, we'll love them unconditionally.

"Funny, right?" Cole asks. "Who would have thought that this is where we would have ended up? Sitting in the backyard, sipping on beer, watching our kids play, while our wives use the excuse of 'making dinner' so they can socialize without the interruption of us or the kids?" He grins.

"Yep," Kacen says, deadpan, and we all chuckle at his reply.

Kacen was always the calm one of the bunch. Never bringing home random girls, he was an old soul, so to speak. Matured beyond his years, he was always ready to settle down and have babies. When I met Logan for the first time and realized she was his girl from the beach, I knew he was sunk.

"Wouldn't change it, brother," Tristan says.

"Nope," the four of us say in unison.

When we first started the band, way back when, I fell into the fame, the girls, and although I'm not proud of that, I'm glad my path led me to her. To my wife and kids. To my band of brothers and their families.

There is nothing like spending time with those you love to Serenade your soul.

CONTACT
KAYLEE RYAN

I cannot thank you enough for taking the time to read Insistent. I appreciate each and every one of you. I'd love to hear from you.

Facebook:
http://bit.ly/2C5DgdF

Reader Group:
http://bit.ly/2O0yWDx

Goodreads:
http://bit.ly/2HodJvx

Twitter:
@author_k_ryan

Instagram:
Kaylee_ryan_author

Website:
www.kayleeryan.com/

ALSO BY
KAYLEE RYAN

With You Series

Anywhere With You

More With You

Everything With You

Stand Alone Titles

Tempting Tatum

Unwrapping Tatum

Levitate

Just Say When

Unexpected Reality

I Just Want You

Reminding Avery

Hey, Whiskey

When Sparks Collide

Pull You Through

Beyond the Bases

Soul Serenade Series

Emphatic

Assured

Definite

Insistent

ALSO BY
KAYLEE RYAN

Southern Heart Series
Southern Pleasure
Southern Desire
Southern Attraction
Southern Devotion

ACKNOWLEDGEMENTS

It's hard to see this series come to an end. In the beginning Emphatic was supposed to be a standalone novel, but you asked for more. It took me some time, but each of the Soul Serenade guys finally have their HEA. Thank you for sticking with me, and following the band ☺

To my readers:

I never thought that anyone would be interested in my stories, you have proved me wrong. I am truly honored to have you on this journey with me. Thank you for always supporting me.

To my family:

I'm blessed beyond measure with the support that you provide. I could not do this without you.

Scott Hoover:

Thank you for an amazing image of Travis. I look forward to working with you again soon.

Tami Integrity Formatting:

You have a way of taking my words and turning them into a beautiful little package. You put up with my changes and my frantic messages. I don't know what I would do without you. As always, it's been amazing and my pleasure working with you.

Travis DesLaurier:

Thank you for doing what you do and being the face of Insistent.

Sommer Stein:

Your talent never ceases to amaze me. Thank you for yet another stunning cover. You've brought this series to life and for that I thank you.

My beta team:

Jamie, Stacy, and Lauren I would be lost without you. You read my words as much as I do, and I can't tell you what your input and all the time you give means to me. Thank you from the bottom of my heart for taking this wild ride with me.

Give Me Books:

With every release, your team works diligently to get my book in the hands of bloggers. I cannot tell you how thankful I am for your services.

Tempting Illustrations:

Thank you for the promotional teasers. You're the best!

Bloggers:

Thank you, doesn't seem like enough. You don't get paid to do what you do. It's from the kindness of your heart and your love of reading the fuels you. Without you, without your pages, your voice, your reviews, spreading the word it would be so much harder if not impossible to get my words in reader's hands. I can't tell you how much your never-ending support means to me. Thank you for being you, thank you for all that you do.

To my Kick Ass Crew:

The name of the group speaks for itself. You ladies truly do KICK ASS! I'm honored to have you on this journey with me. Thank you for reading, sharing, commenting, suggesting, the teasers, the messages all of it. Thank you from the bottom of my heart for all that you do. Your support is everything!

With Love,

Kaylee Ryan
AUTHOR

Made in the USA
Columbia, SC
13 January 2020